In a deft move, a skill Allan had long ago mastered, he swept her into his arms and soundly kissed her pouty lips. A jolt went through him like a blow to the back of his neck. He momentarily lost what his intention had been. He fell into Marissa like a burning log into a grate, and with the same degree of heat.

They parted and gazed at one another.

"See how you are," she mumbled. "A scoundrel and a rakehell."

He brushed off his waistcoat. "And you are a lovely, desirable girl who needed kissing. I cannot apologize, it felt too wonderful."

"Then make it last as a fond memory," she hissed, "because it will never happen again."

That is what you think, Allan confided to himself.

Praise for Jeanette Collins

The Gamble

by

Jeanette Collins

The Gamble

Cover Art by *The Wild Rose Press, Inc.*

The Wild Rose Press, Inc.
PO Box 708
Adams Basin, NY 14410-0708
Visit us at www.thewildrosepress.com

Publishing History
First Edition, 2022
Trade Paperback ISBN 978-1-5092-4519-2
Digital ISBN 978-1-5092-4520-8

Published in the United States of America

Chapter One

Thursday, May 22, 1817

Allan Rutledge stood at a safe distance as the pack of straining horses sped past in a haze of dust, kicking up clods of mud. A man stationed on a platform above him shouted into a bullhorn, "Azor takes it, by haaalf a length! Young Wizard secccc-ond!"

A collective groan swept over the crowd, and Allan mentally joined in. His last hundred pounds had been on Sylvanus, sworn to win by the Duke of Rutland's head trainer. The man, decidedly foxed at the time, talked to anyone who would listen. Once again, Allan should have known better than to rely on the tip.

Allan, moving quickly away from the shuffling throng and to the hack stand, would return to his lodgings and reckon how to get out of this latest financial fix. He rode back to the town High Street in a hack that smelt of horse manure from the boots of others and entered the Corner Inn, where he had stayed for the last few days. The innkeeper, a crafty fellow, gave him a meaningful glance when he entered. The blighter knew the Derby had been run and eyed him, watchful for losers. Allan had joined that group.

"Staying on, sir?" he pointedly inquired, polishing the front window.

"No, I shall depart in the morning."

"Your charges will be ready, sir."

Likely they would be. Allan climbed the stairs, the narrow, uncarpeted hallway redolent of floor wax. In his room, he removed a woolen pouch from his portmanteau and emptied the contents into his hand. A small cameo brooch he favored, the carved image touching; a man's wide gold band; and a more elaborate gold signet ring, set with an emerald and a crest. My lucky charms, he thought ruefully and dropped the band into his waistcoat pocket.

Allan left the building, the innkeeper's gimlet gaze on him, and went along the street to the inevitable pawnbroker's shop. Epsom, a racing town, saw to every need, win or lose. He entered to the dull clang of an overhead bell and faced a gnarled old man with a seamed and furrowed face, greed all over his features like whiskers.

"What might I do fer ye, sor?" he inquired in a voice of doom.

"I wish to sell this," Allan said, placing the ring on the stained wood counter.

The man seized the band and, with a cracked glass, peered at it. "Heavy. Gold over lead, I be thinkin'."

Allan knew better but did not reply.

The oaf cast a perfunctory glance at the ring. The creature bounced it in his paw as Allan studied his expression, noting the little uptick of his mouth. He badly wanted the ring; how much cash did the fellow have?

"Ten pounds," he growled.

Allan merely looked at him, knowing he probably been offered a half.

The man shifted from foot to foot, his eyes still fixed

on the valuable ring. "Fifteen, that be final."

Now Allan spoke. "Twenty."

"See here, sor," he whined. "I got to make me profit."

Allan stood there, again saying nothing. The man clutched the ring in his beefy hand. Then he reached into a drawer and withdrew a scuffed leather purse. He dropped it on the counter, opened it, and dumped out twenty gold sovereigns.

"That is the lot, all I have. Take it and go."

"I would have the purse, if you please," Allan requested.

The man shoved it to him, his expression sullen.

"Thank you." Allan scooped the coins into it. The purse weighty in his coat pocket, he walked out. The ring, worth a lot more, had been no loss to him. He'd won it at cards and had added it to his charms, but so far, it had not brought him any blasted luck. This amount would give him a good evening meal and a decent bottle, pay off the inn, and catch the mail coach back to London not entirely broke. Then he would see if Stubbins had sent along his allowance. High bloody time he did.

****

Friday

The dusty mail coach, both ancient and crowded, smelled of axle grease. Allan gave his case to the driver and climbed aboard, braced to travel with less than desirable companions. Namely a portly lady in a ridiculous floppy hat, a studious reverend, all in black and holding a large bible, and two ladies of questionable station. He fitted himself into a place next to the reverend. The two full-blown lovelies smiled hopefully at him as off they went, the big coach lurching side to side, the morning sun rising like a beacon over the quiet fields. Allan had missed breakfast to catch this early coach, and his stomach growled.

"Been to the races, have ye?" one woman coyly asked, sounding him out.

"Indeed, I have, ma'am, and my choice ran third."

"Aye, that be why you are riding in *this*," the other woman judged, knocking a knuckle on the side of the timeworn vehicle.

"Better it is than walking, I will allow," commented the reverend piously.

"Barely," allowed the woman in the hat.

"I am happy to ride," Allan added, "and it is all I can pay for."

The two women promptly lost interest in him and whispered to each other. Allan sat back, glad to travel in silence. Shortly, they reached Ewell, and to his relief, the lot of them departed. He stepped down for the ensuing minutes it took to see to the skittish team and observed an uncommonly pretty young woman speaking to the burly driver. The man jerked a thumb in the direction of the coach and took her valise. Allan's spirits rose. The girl hesitated, glanced cautiously behind her, then came his way, very much on the alert.

She wore a trim, light-blue carriage dress and a dark-tan straw hat with a white silk flower on the short brim. Glossy red-gold hair curled in tendrils beneath it. Proper gloves, an ample tapestry reticule, and she carried a small, covered basket. She passed by without noticing him and waited at the coach door.

He knew no one would come to help her in, so Allan ambled that direction and offered his hand. "If I may?"

She jumped, her hazel eyes wide.

4

"Help you in? There is no groom." He smiled, aiming to appear inoffensive.

"Thank you," she whispered.

Allan took her small hand and helped her up, catching a subtle whiff of perfume. The light, clean scent made him a little dizzy as he climbed in after her. He took the rear-facing seat, giving her the better vantage of facing forward. She looked about the yard somewhat anxiously, her rosy lips parted.

"This is not so bad," he ventured.

Again surprised, she rather had to locate him in space. "Pardon?"

"Traveling in the mail coach."

"Oh," she said, her voice a pleasing tone. "There is no other way to London from Ewell."

Her clothing and refined manner indicated quality. Allan knew his situation, but what about her? She had run away from something, just like him. With Allan, it had long been recurring debt, the wrong preoccupations, heedless waste, rampant carelessness, blazing irritation, and all the rest. He felt constantly pursued by a band of emotional scalawags, petulant losers, and rapacious creditors.

But this little miss had never so much as squashed a spider. Her presence softened the edges of a hard world. Virtue spread over her like butter on bread. What a change from his usual female contacts. Allan stealthily looked her over, hat to small half boots. Out here, traveling on her own? He highly disapproved. Why no maid?

She continued to gaze worriedly in all directions. He waited for other passengers to arrive, but none came. Zounds! He would have her all to himself for fifteen or so miles, and Allan, a lover of women, reveled in the opportunity. Sure enough, the door banged shut, the driver cracked his whip, the coach pulled forward and soon gained speed. They took the London road. The girl drew a long breath and visibly relaxed, the basket resting on her lap.

Allan detected the warm smell of food; his mouth watered, and his belly pinched. What did she have in that basket? They rode along in the sunshine, the country air brand new. He spoke. "I have been in Epsom. At the Derby. My horse lost, and so did I."

"Ah," she murmured.

"Is Ewell your home?"

"Nearby."

"Good country hereabouts," he remarked.

More silence as they passed farms, fields with grazing cows, and a flock of rather dingy sheep. She gazed absently out the window as if he were not there. Allan thought he had lost ground before he had taken any. She pulled off her gloves, reached into the basket, withdrew a morsel, and popped it into her mouth. Allan endured such a terrible sense of loss it must have shown since she perceived it.

"Your pardon. I had no breakfast," she said.

"Ah," he answered.

She studied him. "Would you care for—"

"Yes, I would. Anything; I too, had no breakfast and am starved."

She uncovered the basket and guilelessly held it forward. Allan saw small sandwiches, cakes, and fruit.

"Have something," she offered.

Allan selected a sandwich and ate it in two bites. She offered another, and he took it. Delicate tea sandwiches, chicken and cucumber. They quietly shared the contents of the basket, Allan struck by her generosity.

"I lost everything at the Derby," he admitted, biting into a juicy raspberry.

She considered this remark while nibbling a sandwich. "Everyone loses at the races, except the owners."

He frowned. What did this girl know about racing? "Well, take into account they must pay for feed, stabling, training, and so on," he informed her. "Racing can become very costly. It is a wealthy man's pastime."

"But win or lose, they retain the horse," she coolly replied, "and surely possess the facilities to keep the animal with others, likely in great comfort. Then they sell their essence."

Allan laughed out loud, but she went on.

"It makes a great deal of pleasure and sport for them as well. They do not heed the losses of those who wager, and to my mind, they run the poor animals to death. Have this last cake?"

Glad to get it, he replied, "I thought I could make a score."

"Everyone thinks that. Gambling creates losers."

Allan flinched. "Eh?"

"I have personally observed gambling to be an affliction. It is the way loss happens. If you stand aside, you can see it control people. Watch them lose and suffer over it."

He should know. "You suffer?" he asked.

"No, they do. I never wager and believe I have no inherent luck."

"I am lucky today," he replied, "to be sharing a coach with a philosopher. I am grateful. May I know your name?"

She shook her head, and bright curls shivered gold. "No."

"Well, is that friendly? My name is Allan, and I assure you, I am totally harmless."

"Oh? Harmless people never say so."

Allan did not know how to respond to this insight. He did know for a girl like her, he could be highly dangerous.

What sort of fellow could this be, Marissa wondered. A bold one. He oozed charm like bees ooze honey. The way he sat, so elegant, so privileged, spoke volumes. He looked to be the indulged son of someone, now reduced to riding the mail. She knew why she had no carriage, but what about him?

In the warmth of the coach, he removed his soft hat, and Marissa liked to observe him. Quite handsome, masculine, and he had fine hands, well cared for, with long fingers.

He had lost his money at the racetrack, so rather a profligate. He was fashionably dressed in fine clothing, and his dark brown hair had been cut by an expert. The carefully tousled style suited him. His eyes were very dark. Too dark to see into, to see *him*, and he likely preferred that.

She had eaten too much. Tossing over bumps in the road began to make her feel woozy. She nervously kept fearing the coach would be overtaken. That the villain would come after her and force her away, no matter what she said or did.

Marissa calmed herself. He could not know; there had not been time for that. No one knew she had left, so he could not find out. Not yet. Then, the warm day, the tension and stress, swept over her. The food sat uneasily in her stomach. The coach rocked over deep ruts, and momentarily dazed, she felt herself slowly begin to slide from the seat.

Large hands gripped her arms and lifted her back. "Easy, be easy."

"So sorry—" she mumbled.

"Nothing to it." He now sat beside her, supporting her with his arm across her shoulders.

Marissa had the impulse to cry, fought it off, and took a deep breath. "I do apologize. I have um, been in a difficult situation, and am quite—overset."

"What are you running away from?" he asked.

Shocked, she breathed, "How did you know?"

"It is evident. By your vigilant attitude, you worry somebody is after you. Your face is flushed, your pulse is beating in your throat. I notice such things."

"Are you a medical man?" she inquired.

"No." He grinned. "I am a gambler."

How awful! Marissa attempted to shrug him off but could not. "I am fine now, thank you."

He eased away some but kept his seat beside her.

"I play cards to live," he related. "I have very little income and strive to make it go around. I must pay my tailor and my bootmaker and keep up a good appearance, suitable to my rank and education as a gentleman."

"Oh, mercy," she groaned.

"Generally, one or more creditors are on my trail, so I can spot the signs. Whom do you owe?"

"No creditors." Marissa arranged her words. "Others seek to call in an unfair obligation."

He nodded sagely. "Family, of course. It usually is. What demands have they made?"

She studied him. Marissa wanted very much to speak, to tell someone. Did she dare? Strong emotions overtook her. "I am to be sold off!" she cried.

He stared, obviously taken aback.

"It is a long story," she added.

"I would hear it."

Marissa sighed, worn out with no one to speak to about her problem. The whole of it clamored to be told. Where to start?

"Ours is an old house," she began. "Quite old, in fact, but sturdy enough. Four years ago, my father became convinced that under the west foundation, Norman treasure had been buried, hidden by his ancestors." The story tumbled out. "A badge set into the stones held symbols that said so, accompanied by a dire curse should it be disturbed. Widely thought to be a jolly tale, everyone let it go as a legend. Not my father. Work began, requiring the west wall to be heavily supported, and they began to remove stones."

"Not a good decision," he guessed.

It upset her all over again. "Exactly! A third of the wall fell down. Unfazed, Father went on. More workmen came, the job enlarged, and soon it all began to eat large quantities of funds. The house became drafty and chill, my father's secretary warned of substantial financial risk, then resigned, and it became a complete disaster."

Marissa let it all out. "Father's mind could not be changed; he had become obsessed. Precious artworks and tapestries were gradually sold to pay for this folly. Soon, merchants showed up at the kitchen door demanding their charges. Chaos all around, the money disappeared like morning fog." She twisted the strings of her reticule. "Everything fell apart. I had no come out.

This will be my first time in London."

Marissa glanced at him. He listened, his expression genial. Might as well say the rest. "But I received more woe. Early this year, I began to have an unwanted, persistent, and demanding caller."

"Oh, no," he murmured, his expression concerned.

"An obnoxious, ghastly man. I learned abruptly, only yesterday, that my father had allowed him to ask for my hand. In fact, contracts were being drawn up, and upon the marriage, Father would receive five thousand pounds. I declined forcefully, but nothing could be done. He wanted the money for his quest. A lot more than he wanted me." Marissa sat tall, despite his long arm, which had returned. "So, this morning, I ran away."

He gave her a hug. "Good!"

She did not complain. "Yes. I have a great-aunt in London. I hope to stay there until, well, until I am sure I am free of him. Because I fear the terrible man will attempt to force the issue."

"The bounder!" he exclaimed, his expression righteous.

Unexpectedly, Marissa laughed, easing her tension, and felt better.

What a sweetheart, Allan marveled. How long had it been since he had encountered such a spunky girl? He had sunk into a pit of decadence some time back. She did not cry or fuss, simply stated the facts. Allan liked this feisty rustic.

"I would say you are worth more than five thousand," he assured her. "Ten, easily. Come now. Tell me your name."

"Marissa."

"Ah. Meaning 'of the sea.' "

"I have never seen the sea and wish to do so," she eagerly stated. "And all the sights of London, if my aunt will allow."

"All by yourself? Where is your maid?"

"One cannot run away with a maid," she scoffed, "and no friend to me, she told Father everything. Both she and my clothes can be replaced. I will buy other garments, of my own choosing."

Interesting. "Have you sufficient funds for this indulgence?"

She gripped her reticule. "I do."

By the Gods! "Traveling alone?" Allan inquired. "I trust this is not on your person?"

"Indeed not. When life started to come to pieces, I began to set money aside for myself. Almost like wages, for keeping the household together. In three years," she declared proudly, "I have accumulated a draft for five hundred pounds."

Despite good intentions, Allan began to plan how to relieve her of some of it. Dastardly, he scolded himself, unacceptable. "Well," he advised, "do not play cards with anyone. Guard your funds. The future is uncertain."

"I will not resort to wagering, even though"—she gestured aimlessly—"I am taking the gamble that I can survive. And that I am not risking great loss. But I simply had to leave, do you not agree?"

"Yes, I do. Staying would have led to misery."

"Yessss." She sighed and looked closely at him. "Misery."

Allan gazed into her hazel eyes and saw flecks of gold and green. With her red-gold hair, she presented a feast for the eyes. Such a country girl, on the loose in London, filled him with dread. What would happen to

12

her, a stripling among sharks? And what the blazes could he do about it?

The vehicle bowled along the better road. Marissa sat back, comforted to have told her story and to have this Allan agree she had been right to leave. A most interesting person. He sat too close; they had never been introduced, but who cared? She would never see him again, a gambler and likely notorious. Women all over the city and whatnot. With that face and manner, he would attract ladies like dust to a corner. And he had extremely long legs. She found this most interesting. His arm around her seemed very friendly and supportive, then he gave her another little hug. She caught a breath. How daring of him!

"So," she said, moving away slightly. "You have business in London?"

"Very little, but I live there."

Marissa considered this. "Do you mean you have no occupation?"

"I told you. I am a gambler."

"Well," she objected, "you cannot do that all the time."

He nodded. "Correct. I only gamble when I have no money."

"But—"

"As I said, I have a meager income. When that runs low, I play cards."

Marissa considered him a rogue. "I do hope you are more fortunate at cards than you were at the races."

"My dear," he said with a wink, "I assure you I am. How do you propose to make *your* way in the world?"

"I have many excellent abilities," she bragged. "I can do bookkeeping, run a large household, deal with tradesmen and servants, speak idiomatic French, and play the pianoforte with some skill."

"What," he teased, "no drawing abilities?"

"Enough to render a likeness," she added. "No easy task."

"Mmmm. These are the qualities of a good man's wife, rich or poor. However, they are not worth tuppence in the marketplace."

"I will learn what I need to know," she confidently asserted.

"Dancing is a worthy skill to acquire," he mused. "Fine needlework and the like."

Marissa's temper sparked. "What an assumption, you beast, to consider such trifles! I am a worthy person right now. There will be a place for me in London, and I will find it."

He smiled shrewdly. "I would hire you, Miss Marissa."

She leaned away. "Really? In what capacity?"

"Companion and friend. I do not need a bookkeeper; my household is small. I encounter few tradesmen, have only a threadbare valet, speak fluent French, and do not at present own a pianoforte. But I get lonely, and you are a lovely woman. I could show you the wonders of London."

"Oh, could you?" she suspiciously inquired. "I did not hear compensation mentioned in that litany."

"Share and share alike, I say."

Marissa shook her head. "Undependable, I fear. Half of nothing is nothing."

"I feel the same," he wearily said. "Yet, on I go."

He sounded so cavalier, she had to smile. "Add to that, if you are lonely, I am Queen Mary."

He inclined his tousled head. "I caught the resemblance, Your Highness."

She poked his arm with a finger. "You would attract women like lint to velvet."

He laughed handsomely. "What an image. Crowds of women run after my favors?"

"A true tale, I am sure."

"And you?" he countered. "How many lovers did you entertain before you jumped the fence?"

"Lovers?" she cried. "How dare you imply—"

"Tut-tut. You assumed that I am a gigolo."

"I did not! I hardly know what that is."

"Good, because I am not one. I have never taken a shilling from a woman."

"I never thought you would! I had in mind an, um, that you were perhaps—a London rake."

"A rake, is it?" he questioned with some ire. "If I were indeed such a man, I would have had you thoroughly beguiled by now, alone in a coach with your emotions out on stalks. And you would never have seen it coming. The idea! If I had charge of you, Miss Marissa, you would be shackled to a keeper, preferably a eunuch."

Her mouth dropped open at such a scenario. "Well!" she huffed. "Thank goodness you are not in charge of me. I would just as soon go back to the duke."

He raised a brow. "What duke?"

"The monster who demands to marry me."

"By heaven!" he exclaimed, clutching his chest. "You refused a *duke*?"

"You are nutty in the head," Marissa said, turning to the window and crossing her arms defiantly. "It is useless to talk to you."

Allan became impressed. The girl had some pluck.

"Now, do not get your hackles up, Marissa. It is just that there is little opportunity for a gentlewoman, which I am sure you are, to earn. I cannot see you scrubbing floors. Therefore."

She turned back to him. "Therefore what?" she questioned.

He shrugged. "I do not know. It will require thought."

"I have thought. I mean to look about, learn the city, and see what I may do."

What planet had she fallen from? "Who are you, Marissa? Give me your surname. This treasure-hunter papa is whom?"

Silence.

"You imagine I will get back to him?" Allan assumed a furtive pose, speaking behind his hand. " 'Oh, by the by, good sir,' I might say, 'I accompanied your daughter to London. We were all alone in a coach, and I ate her sandwiches.' That would go over nicely, eh? I might be given a small reward for your safe return."

"As you drag me back by the hair?" she thundered. "All for crass profit?"

"I recall you are worth five thousand pounds, my pretty. I could make use of such a sum."

She glared fiercely. "Do not even consider it."

"Very well. I will keep your secrets for the price of a kiss."

"I certainly—"

In a deft move, a skill Allan had long ago mastered, he swept her into his arms and soundly kissed her pouty lips. A jolt went through him like a blow to the back of his neck. He momentarily lost what his intention had been. He fell into Marissa like a burning log into a grate, and with the same degree of heat.

They parted and gazed at one another.

"See how you are," she mumbled. "A scoundrel and a rakehell."

He brushed off his waistcoat. "And you are a lovely, desirable girl who needed kissing. I cannot apologize, it felt too wonderful."

"Then make it last as a fond memory," she hissed, "because it will never happen again."

That is what you think, Allan confided to himself.

Traffic increased, and carts, drays, and carriages jostled for space. The big mail coach maneuvered its way through the ragged outskirts of London, the heaving masses on all sides.

Allan watched Marissa absorb the sights. Her expression changed from wonder to surprise to startled appraisal. She withdrew a small handkerchief from her reticule and covered her nose against the stench of humanity. In one corner, embroidered in pink, was a fancy B. Marissa B. He sorted through names he knew but could make no connection. The more he thought about it, her identity became a tantalizing game.

Bentley, Brown, Baker, Bruce? "Biggerstaff," he guessed.

She tore her gaze from the window. "Pardon?"

"Your last name."

"No."

"Boxley, Brewster, Belton, Boarhide?"

"Oh, stop. You did not tell me *your* last name."

"Should I?" he questioned. "After all this time alone, I may claim to be compromised. You did kiss me. Therefore, I shall not reveal myself until under the protection of my solicitor."

"Folderol. I am the one kissed, and I will deny everything you allege. So, what is it?"

"You first."

She squirmed. "Why does everything have to go your way?"

"I am the male."

Up went her hands. "Glory be! I had not noticed."

He relented. "Allan Rutledge, at your service."

"How do you do? I am Marissa Barrington."

"Delighted."

"Well, that is over," she stated. "No more surprises."

"Those are to come," Allan promised, as her attention went back to the window. What would he do with her, and why should he feel responsible? He had a lot on his mind and sixteen gold sovereigns and change to his name. He had to get busy. Damn Stubbins if he had not sent the pittance he had been forced to exist on.

The coach crawled through the busy streets and at last turned into the Star Inn near Portman Square. The place teemed with coaches and assorted vehicles, passengers coming and going, the air full of cries and raucous noise.

Marissa flattened to the seat, her hazel eyes large.

"Not to worry," Allan said, "just city sounds. You will get used to it."

He opened the door and stepped down to see about his portmanteau. Her valise had been put with his. Allan turned back to help her down, but there she stood beside him.

"Shall I find you a hackney?" he inquired politely.

She looked blank.

"A hired vehicle. To take you to your aunt's."

"Oh, yes." She rummaged in her reticule and

withdrew a paper. "I wish to go to number 220 Adam's Row. Do you know if that is far?"

"Too far to walk. A hack is in order." Allan considered her situation. "One moment. Do you have money to pay?"

"I have five shillings, sixpence in coins."

Damnation, he could not just leave her. "Come along, I will see you there. I am going that way."

"Oh, thank you, Allan."

His name in her voice gave him an unexpected shiver. He picked up the cases, offered his arm, and she took it. Allan steered her away from the mob and spotted a decent-looking hack. He marched toward it, thinking himself a fool to get entangled with this loose female.

Allan addressed the jarvey, a rickety-looking fellow in a tattered wool cap. "Ho, there. We are going to— what did you say, Marissa?"

"220 Adam's Row."

The man touched his cap. "In a tot, guv. Step up."

Allan squeezed in the luggage, settled Marissa, and climbed in. Off they went, the girl spellbound by the city. Her expression rapt, her demeanor ladylike, her manner endearing. He glanced aside. Must get shed of this chit. He would unload her at the aunt's and be on his way. If the place seemed proper. She would be fine. Definitely not his problem!

His gaze once more fastened on her lovely face. How delicate she seemed in the grime and harried haste of the city. Of course, she must be a lady of some standing. Dukes were not known to marry just anybody, plus she worried that with his power and connections, he would come after her. For all of that, Allan would never let her go, either. If she were his.

Preposterous. He had blasted little to offer any woman. Better take the duke, little miss, he thought sternly, and eat every day. Allan surprised himself. Jesus, he had become thoroughly jaded.

They crossed Oxford Street, passed Grosvenor Square, and went on another block to Adam's Row. The hack stopped in front of a tall, narrow house of whitened brick with red shutters and a patch of garden in a riot of bloom.

"Is this it?" Allan inquired.

She squinted. "It is number 220."

He twitched. "Wait. You have never been here before?"

"No."

His irritation flared. "Does she know you are coming?"

"I did not have time to write," she murmured.

Now what? Allan opened the door. "Let us just inquire if the lady is at home." He helped Marissa down and told the driver to wait. Up the walk they went, Allan detecting a growing chill in his belly.

When they reached the porch, his worst fears surfaced. Drapes were drawn closed, the area unswept, everything silent and empty of life. The knocker was missing.

Marissa, startled to find no one at home, staggered, painfully chastened. What a fool she had been, as if the whole city would open to her like magic. She had taken it all for granted, had not planned anything, and only escaped to yet another dilemma. Tears rose in her throat.

"No one is here," Allan complained.

How mortifying. "I can see that. I am so sorry. I had no idea and have been stupid." She turned away to go back to the hackney, covered in shame.

"Hold on, Marissa. We will ask next door. They may know when your aunt will return."

"Oh, good idea." She hurried off the porch and across the grass to the other narrow house, Allan trailing. There, some breathless, she dropped the knocker. They waited. Presently, the door swung open, and a footman appeared.

"Good day," Marissa said. "We came to visit Lady Harley next door but found her not at home. Would you—"

His place was taken by a stiffish butler, who droned, "Yessss?"

"I am Lady Harley's niece. She is away. Do you know when she will return?"

The man's nostrils flared in a quick sniff. "Lady Harley, miss, is in Bath for the cure. She is said to return on the twenty-sixth, which is the coming Monday, to retrieve her *cat*," he sneered, "which has us at sixes and sevens." He then bent forward and appeared hopeful. "Perhaps you could rescue us from the howling animal?"

"No, sorry. I am up from the country and have nowhere—well, thank you."

Marissa reeled off the porch and stumbled into Allan's arms. She must decide what to do next; she must have money. "Perhaps," she suggested, "I could go to the bank and cash my draft?"

He hustled her along the walk. "I would like better to have tea and lots to eat. It has been a trying day, Marissa."

"Well, then," she murmured, thoroughly defeated. "Thank you. I could not ask you for more. If I may take the hackney—"

Allan tipped back his jaunty felt hat. "No, no. I cannot have you wandering the streets. We will go to my digs."

She paused at the hack door. "Pardon?"

"My residence. Driver, 302 Dover Street, please. Get in, Marissa."

She did so, not knowing what else to do. They took seats. "Is it far?" she anxiously inquired.

"No, and if my valet has not absconded with the plate, I can make you reasonably comfortable. Then we can think how to proceed."

Marissa sat there as if frozen as the vehicle crawled away. How could she have been so ignorant? Panic had taken over her brain, that is what. Cold terror that her life would be stolen, with her father's consent. Sold off like a prize horse, so he could tear down their home and the duke could slaver over her. Better to die.

Speaking of that end, where would this Allan take her? Oh, God. Perhaps she would now be sold to Egyptians. Carried across the world to a terrible fate. A gambler, he would bargain her away to them for—she must stop thinking such things. No one with his polished manners and handsome face would do anything so horrid. Would he? Surely not. He had been excessively kind. Gratitude welled up in her breast.

"When I cash my draft, Allan, I will give you a part."

He turned to her, his expression puzzled. "What?"

"For helping me. I do not have much, but you said you have lost all your money, so I would like to share. Until, well, until we have more."

Chapter Two

We, Allan silently repeated. *We*? The daffodil thought they were we? Then he quickly became abashed. She would give him a portion of what little she possessed? Glory, a wandering saint.

"Marissa, I must decline, but you are most generous, and I am obliged. However, I assume funds are pending, although my solicitor, with whom I am forced to deal, is dilatory of late. I am confident that when we reach home, he will have come through with my allowance."

"You have an allowance?" she marveled.

"An insulting percentage, make no mistake; a remnant, a scrap."

"Such a shame," she said in genuine sympathy. Unexpectedly, Allan loved this.

The hack stopped at his latest home. He stepped down, retrieved the luggage, and helped Marissa alight. She gazed about, up to the fine house, then to him.

"I will pay for the hackney," she offered.

Tempted, Allan refused. He paid, took the baggage, and they trotted up the walk to a square of porch. He let them in with his key and dropped the cases. His valet came jogging down the stairs, his large frame moving lightly.

"Oh, sir," he cried, with some urgency, then took in the scene. "Good afternoon."

"Murray. We are starved and need tea immediately.

This is my uh, friend, Miss…" He fumbled for her name. "…Burlington."

The woman smiled, lighting up the hall. "That is Barrington, if you please, Murray. Our acquaintance is recent."

Murray, visibly bewildered to have been addressed, said, "Yes, Miss Barrington."

"We will have that tea in the drawing room."

"Yes, sir." The man paused. "If I might have a word?"

"Later. Did Stubbins call by?"

"Oh, yes, sir, he did, and that is why I need—"

Allan smiled, much relieved. "In good time, Murray. Bring tea and food."

The valet hastened away.

"Come along, Marissa," he said, taking her arm and escorting her to the drawing room. He parked her on a settee, added logs to the fire, and sat down across from her.

"This is a very beautiful house," she observed.

"It is not mine. My friend is in Boston for some months, and I am on duty."

She glanced around the luxurious room. "Where did you live before?"

His empty stomach growled rather loudly. "At an inn not far from here. I came down from Oxford three years ago and, needs must, got comfortable enough there."

"God save me," she whispered. "Oxford?"

"I lingered and took a second degree since not required to be anywhere. I had little else to do. Quite soon after, I had very little of anything. Therefore, the gambling."

"What happened?"

The question overwhelmed him. He quickly became freshly enraged, but with fortitude, calmed himself. "I quarreled with my guardian." He took a steadying breath. "He accused me of a grave offense I did not commit. I objected, things escalated, and he cut me off with—"

Murray entered the room bearing a tray, placed it on a low table, and silently withdrew. Allan pounced on a beef sandwich, chewed, and gestured impatiently to the teapot.

Marissa poured and handed him a cup, her gaze on him. It made him cross. Allan did not like to be questioned and had told her more than he intended. Vexing in the extreme.

She went off on another tangent, balancing her teacup. "Does Murray do everything?"

"Yes. The staff have been given leave. He is an able man."

"How unusual. Where did you find him?"

Damn her and her questions. "I won him."

Those serious hazel eyes regarded him.

"He had been unhappy in his position, and when the man who employed him wagered carelessly, Murray came to work for me."

She gazed soulfully at him. Allan could not stand it. "And if I go to risky places," he stated grumpily, "Murray watches out for me."

"He is a bodyguard," she evenly said.

How would she know such a thing? "Yes, he is. Never say so to him," he requested. "Murray is a sensitive man."

She sipped her tea. "I believe so are you."

Allan fumed. "Ridiculous. Hard as nails, with a

heart of leather."

She just smiled again. He remembered kissing those full, pink lips. He would like to thrash her, then kiss her again. Really kiss her. Allan took another sandwich, bit in and chewed, his calculating gaze on her.

Marissa now had a few points with which to gauge his borders. Oxford, so impressive. His *friend* owned this deluxe house. Allan had a protective valet/bodyguard, that he won at cards. It all came right out of a novel! He had scant resources, so he gambled, but did not seem devious and cunning, her idea of a gaming man. However, he had remained throughout today irritable, quick to change his mood, rather imperious, and very bright, from the way he used language. And he had a full set of armor in place. He should clank when he walked.

He must surely be annoyed to have her around his neck, so to speak, but what could she do? Tomorrow she would resume command of her own life, cash the draft, and find a place to stay. It could all be done. But what about tonight? She sipped her tea, a tasty brew, and found Allan unusually beautiful to look at.

The more Marissa observed him, the better he became, a storybook prince type of thing. The way his dark hair fell across his brow and his dark, dark eyes made her throat feel overwarm when he gazed at her. He kept himself contained, and to her, it seemed to be of long habit.

The light in the fine room changed, and the encroaching evening began to trouble her. After this tea, she would take her leave. Marissa tried to devise a plan but faced a great void.

"Eat something, Marissa," he urged. "You will be refreshed if you do. Take this last sandwich. It is thin-sliced beef, one of Murray's specialties."

She chose it and had a bite. It tasted very good, so she had another bite, and chewed. The sandwich disappeared. She had more tea, and Allan ate everything else on the tray. Marissa could not take her eyes from him. He sat there, totally male, mysterious, and entirely from another world. A world she knew nothing of.

What a tight spot he had gotten into, Allan grieved. Friday, no auntie until Monday, and it seemed crystal clear the waif would not be up to negotiating the city. Saturday and Sunday loomed until he could be done with her.

Allan drank more tea and scowled at Marissa, gracefully sitting there. He had to admit she aggravated him with her tempting innocence. Her prim little blue gown churned up visions of her without it. The straw hat with the droopy silk flower struck him as utterly feminine, and likely, she knew it. Of course, she did! That gorgeous face and searing red and gold hair. A mantrap. Trouble in half boots.

She smiled brilliantly, and transfixed, he immediately forgot all of it.

"It is most kind of you to help me, Allan. I know I have become a burden. This inn you mentioned— perhaps they would have a room for me?"

Allan remembered the musty smells in the hallway. The noise in the taproom, the shady drinkers, the festering danger of men looking for a quick dodge. The thought of Marissa there gave him the jitters.

"It is not a place for a lady, Marissa. Actually, nowhere is safe for a woman on her own. Not a woman like you," he grumbled.

She gaped. "What is the matter with me?"

Loony girl. "Do you own a mirror? A legion of men would fall on you, alone, with no one to watch out for you. A public inn is out of the question." Her expression clouded. If she began to cry—swallowing his irritation, Allan declared, "You will stay here tonight."

She resisted. "Whaaat? Certainly, I cannot. It would raise a scandal if I did so."

"With whom? We have been alone together all day. Scandal has multiplied, but neither of us is a prisoner of society, so who could object? You need a place, and there are a number of bedrooms here besides mine."

She bit her lower lip, giving him a shiver. "What about Murray?"

"Murray is harmless. If he should make an offensive move, I will kill him. Can you get by with no maid?"

"Yessss—"

"Then stay." A grin escaped him, thinking of her nearby. "Remember that I am harmless, too," he fibbed.

Doubtful, she replied, "Well, sir, perhaps I am not. *I* may steal the plate."

Allan had to laugh at the saucy child. "How old are you?" he asked.

"Twenty." A long pause. "In two months."

Allan stared, appalled. An infant on the loose!

"How old are you?" she asked with apparent interest.

"Four and twenty. Therefore, you must listen to me, a wise older man." An idea occurred to him to take her mind off things. "If you are good, tomorrow, I will take you about town to see the sights."

Her pretty face lit up. "Would you? I would love that."

"Excellent, that is all settled. Wait here, and I will

speak to Murray about arrangements."

He quit the room and went in search of Murray, found downstairs in the kitchen, watching a pot on the fire, the place evocative of cooked onion.

"Murray, the girl has nowhere safe to go and is staying the night here. Can you fix up a room?"

"Yes sir, but I must say—"

Allan held up a staying hand. "It is most unconventional for a lady, I know, but her aunt is away until Monday and—"

Murray appeared strangely agitated.

"What the devil is the matter?"

"Oh, sir, I have hard news," he murmured in a grave tone. The man smoothed his apron. "I regret to say, sir, that your relation, Mr. Eban Newton, has died."

Shocked, Allan gaped wordlessly.

"Mr. Stubbins informed me only yesterday, sir. I am sorry for your loss."

Allan gasped, "What happened?"

"It seems his carriage crashed at a high speed." Murray clasped his big hands together. "I must tell you his wife is gone as well."

Allan swayed, thunderstruck. The old bitch, too? Beyond imagination. He felt shaky with a sudden, guilt-free joy and leaned on the wall.

Murray lamented. "Most tragic, sir. Mr. Stubbins is anxious to talk with you before you go down to the Hall."

Yes, yes, he must go. Allan could scarcely believe it. No more gambling, no more pinching every coin, wrongly accused and shut out from everything rightfully his.

"I will go to Stubbins first thing, Murray. Thank you. Amazing." He had to ask again. "Both gone, you say?"

"Yes, sir," Murray answered dolefully, his long face dejected.

Allan squeezed the good man's muscled arm. "Not to worry, my friend. We will survive and prosper. Is there dinner?"

"A roasted fowl, sir. All is in order for seven."

"Perfect. And the room?"

"Right away, sir."

Allan wanted to hug the valet but did not. "Murray, you are a priceless gem. Not to fear, this event will benefit the both of us." Allan hurried away, his mind spinning, the astonishing news thrumming through his brain. His cruel and vindictive guardian and his hateful wife were dead, and Allan strutted, quite unpredictably liberated.

Allan returned to the drawing room, his mind occupied, and faced Marissa. Habitual caution and suspicion of others seized him. He went on guard. Jesus, did she somehow know of this, no, *these* deaths? Maybe, a practiced fortune hunter, she had gotten in that coach to seduce him in some way. He had forgotten to ask Murray when the divine accident had occurred. Then she gazed up at him with such an open, outgoing expression, he felt like a heel. She had moved to the sofa near the fire. Allan sat down with her, figuring out what to say. Better to say nothing.

"Dinner at seven, Murray promised," he told her, "and he will arrange your room accordingly."

"Thank you, that is most kind." She rose. "I should not impose on you further."

Blasted woman. "Sit down, Marissa. The room is not ready yet. What about dinner?"

She sat down. "I am just so ashamed to have been imprudent and to land in your lap. I am usually a fairly reasonable person, but in truth, I panicked and left home as soon as I could, to catch that mail coach." Her hazel eyes glistened with unshed tears. "And how truly fortunate to meet you. I now know I would not have been at all prepared. I am a foolish bumpkin."

Allan, touched, had to smile. She had not landed in his lap, but he would welcome it. "No need to worry, Marissa. Your first time out in the world, I gather. A person has to learn as best they can. Buck up! We are friends now, right?"

"Oh, I hope so."

"Then think no more of it. Have a sherry?"

"Yes, thank you."

He got up to pour the drinks. If she thanked him again, he would—but how sweet of her. His temper rose. Why had he never met such a woman? Of course, he had not looked. Bitter and hostile, he had retreated socially and spent his evenings in the company of coarse men and louche women. He *never* had to go back, he realized in a cresting wave of mirth.

Allan returned with the drinks, the news too great, too astounding, not to share, and handed her a glass. Sat down beside her and said, "Murray has given me momentous news."

Marissa, expectant, turned to him.

"My guardian," he began, uncertain how to characterize the bastard, "who financially constrained me for a number of years, has suddenly died."

"Oh!" She regarded him. "But this death does not distress you?"

She'd read his mind, or something. "Not a whit. Not

a crumb."

"That is too bad," she sadly remarked. "He is now beyond you, and no reparation can be made. Nor can your anger be resolved."

"Why should it be?" he crossly demanded.

"Because it will likely be a blight on your life. Better that you should forgive him. Not for his sake, but for yours."

Allan seethed. Had the chit invaded from another universe? "That is very virtuous, my dear," he wryly commented, "but it happens I have a rougher edge than you."

Marissa sipped the sherry. "I knew it would only hurt me to hate my father for what he did. I pushed it aside; I had a lot to handle in my small life. The house began to fall down around me. I existed in fear, beset by tradesmen, as one by one, then finally in a group, the servants quit."

She became rebellious, her hazel eyes flashed. "I cooked, cleaned, and did laundry while Father raved, but I held on to myself," the girl asserted. "My real, deep-down self, or I would have collapsed under the load I carried. Hatred would have crippled my efforts. I am sorry he injured you, Allan. It must have hurt you very badly."

Damn, Allan would burst into tears if she kept on. To distract her, he asked, "What about your mother in all this?"

Her open countenance changed to sorrow. "Mother died of a fever when I had almost reached fifteen. We were all devastated; it happened very fast. Father fell to pieces and walked around as if lost. That went on for some time." Marissa sighed deeply. "Then he went crazy."

Allan downed his sherry, unable to comprehend such bravery and strength in a slip of a girl.

His unloved guardian had obviously held the purse strings, Marissa reckoned, and as well, the man had unjustly accused Allan of some awful thing. Arrogant pride surrounded him like a barrier, so such an insult would cut him to the bone. He was firmly that manner of man, anyone could see. Now he would probably have more money, and that would change everything. Money always changed people if they had none, so what would he do now he had become better off? What did it matter, if he could find happiness?

Important things would come along to decide, and that would make his life. As decisions had made hers. Or at least, she had begun the process.

Marissa savored the sherry. Very fine quality, an amontillado, likely. It tasted Spanish, a land she had never seen but had often imagined. Marissa had imagined every place in the world, all in books. Please, God, she prayed, do not let Father destroy the library.

She felt his steady gaze. Why did Allan keep staring at her? She touched her hair and remembered she had not removed her hat. "I must look a fright after such a day."

He gazed at her so directly and for such a long time, Marissa became embarrassed.

"You look fine to me," he at last said. "You are a very attractive woman, so you can do without constant primping." He frowned. "A thing many women are wont to do."

To Marissa, this remark indicated a bad view. "Really, Allan. Do you dislike women?"

He shrugged. "As a group, perhaps; not

individually."

"How disrespectful," she chided. "Lounging about in gambling establishments cannot have brought you into contact with suitable ladies."

"Lounging about?" he protested, with an even deeper frown.

"No one stands up to play cards."

Allan laughed heartily.

Murray tapped at the door and peeped in. "Miss Barrington's room has been prepared, sir. First door to the right of the landing. I took up the valise."

"Very good, Murray."

The man retreated.

"Clear directions, Marissa. Care to go up now?"

"Yes, I would."

"Come along, then."

In the foyer, she looked up the immense stairs, which disappeared into vast darkness.

Allan took a lamp from the entry table. "I'll show you up; it is darker than a coal mine. I am sorry not to offer you the services of a maid," he remarked, as they began to climb.

"I can manage."

They reached the landing and proceeded down a hall to the first door. Allan opened it and light poured out from lamps and a screened, blazing fire.

Marissa turned to him. "If I say thank you again, you will become bored."

He breathed a laugh. "Come down when you will." He turned and walked away, and Marissa entered the room, glad to see a sturdy lock on the door.

Allan trotted back down the stairs, feeling at once free of her and deprived. In the drawing room, he poured a large whiskey and glanced at the indentation in the sofa cushion where she had leaned. He had to get rid of her. She messed with him, with his mind, planting seeds of something debilitating. The girl would drag him down, take up valuable time, and he had a lot to do. It fully hit him that now he would have the estate to manage, in a place he had not lived for years.

What had Eban, or worse, the witch Cordelia, done to the place? Whatever havoc had been raised, Allan felt confident he could fix it, no matter how long it took. He sipped the whiskey; it tore a path down his gullet and stirred his senses. Which were already growing feverish.

Allan very much wanted the woman upstairs. Physically and mentally. All of her. Unadvisable. Now he would have his money, plus the final *allowance*—he despised the word—and could stash her at Mivart's. No one could object to the best hotel in London. A couple of nights there, and boom, the auntie and her cat would take over. This did not cheer him up as much as he had expected.

He had to speak with Stubbins, then get down to Kent and Rutledge Hall. A radical thought occurred. Why not take Marissa with him? That would brighten up the trip, and she would be impressed by the estate. If damnable Eban had not carved it up and cut down all the trees. And it would save his money; Mivart's would be pricey. His mood sank. God in heaven, he had become a miser. Allan must learn all over again how to be rich.

****

The efficient Murray had made the room warm and welcoming. Marissa sat down in a comfy wingchair to catch her breath. It had been the most adventurous day of her existence. She had reached the great metropolis in

Jeanette Collins

the company of a handsome, dashing gambler. Who could credit it? And nothing over, tonight she would sleep in his house. Never mind his distant friend Allan lived here. She thought him rather wonderful, bold and commanding. And a tad grumpy.

She must unpack before her gowns were hopelessly creased. The valise stood nearby. Marissa unlatched it and withdrew the simple gowns she had packed thinking of her elderly aunt, wanting to appear modest. Still, they were nice enough, and she longed to change. She carried them to the dressing room, amazed to find four fabulous dresses hanging there. Gowns such as she had never seen, of silks and satins, in lovely, muted colors.

The lady of the house wore these? Or not. They looked unworn, and one of them had a dressmaker's tag pinned to it. She hung up her gowns and finding water at the washstand, bathed her hands and face. Everything most convenient; surely someone used this room. She walked back to a dressing table by the windows. A silver-backed brush and comb lay there. She examined a cut-glass perfume bottle with a heavy stopper. Marissa smelled it—woodsy. Expensive.

Saints above. Allan had a mistress? She had not asked if he had a wife! Ghastly either way. No, no, four new dresses meant little. Maybe his friend had a sister. She checked the drawers in the chest. Empty. Well. Mighty strange. She ignored the implications, sat down at the dressing table, removed pins, brushed out her long hair, and refashioned it. A tiresome task since she had too much hair.

Marissa returned to the dressing room to choose a gown and studied the lavish dresses. Such elegance. She felt the lovely fabrics. Who would know if she tried one on? She chose the pale rose silk, stepped into it, adjusted, and by golly, it fit fairly well. Although the neckline plunged very low, giving her a moment's pause. Perhaps the latest style, she reasoned. She waltzed out, feeling like royalty, and the glass confirmed her notion. She looked perfectly splendid.

Marissa endured a sharp pang. No come out, never a gown such as this, no good times, no beaux. All for that disgusting treasure that did not exist! Father had knocked down her house, robbed her of security, and she had descended into near poverty and domestic servitude. Then! Sold to that slimy duke. Cruelly unfair and hugely painful.

She stepped to the valise and removed her leather slippers. Pushed off her half boots and put on the slippers. One last look in the glass, and Marissa left the room, righteous as the apostles.

****

Allan changed for dinner, then descended to the drawing room. Empty. Where had she gotten to? Then he heard the rustle of silk, turned, and she drifted down the stairs, coming toward him like a pale flower in bloom. His throat dried. The back of his neck tingled.

He felt a stab of pure rage. Why did he have no one? Cheated out of his life, of ease, of pleasure. Robbed of a woman like Marissa and a house like this. Forced into the gutter to make his way, striving to remain half decent. Allan had barely survived, and it had marked him.

They faced one another. "Very pretty," he muttered.

"You, too," she said, glancing over his evening clothes.

"I have to groom myself to get into exclusive clubs."

"I would admit you." She twirled around. "I found

this gown hanging in the dressing room. It made me envious. I never had such a lovely thing. So, I tried it on. Then, I did not want to take it off again." She tilted her head. "Does it belong to your mistress?"

God, she said things right out. "I do not have a mistress. I cannot afford one."

"Or you would?" she inquired, her expression uncertain.

"Probably not. I do not care to purchase intimate friends."

"Oh, good. That would be demeaning and beneath you."

He absorbed this judgement. "Care for a brandy?" he asked.

"Yes, thank you."

Allan filled two small glasses, handed one to Marissa, and they sat on the settee by the fire.

She sipped the brandy. Allan waited for her to cough and choke. She did not.

"Mmmm. Very nice. Armagnac, I would say. A very full flavor." She took a substantial drink.

Amazed, he asked, "How do you know such a thing?"

"My father enjoyed the best, while I peeled potatoes. I tasted everything, then wanting to know more, I read a book. I remember whatever I read."

Allan became competitive. "Oh, do you?"

"Yes. After a time, it sort of clutters up my mind, and I begin to dismiss things. To make room."

He could scarcely believe his ears. "That is the damnedest, pardon me, a most astounding talent. I, too, have an excellent memory," he boasted. "I have made considerable money being able to remember cards as they are dealt and judging the odds of what remains in the deck. In vingt-et-un, you play against the dealer. It requires staying focused, to say the least."

"I see. I never played that, but I did play loo with the servants. Until they left."

Loo! Allan had to tamp down a sudden, powerful desire for this astonishing woman. She must be his or he would face the blistering Dragon of Loss. "Really," he drawled. "We must have a game."

"Do you think me silly?" she questioned, her hazel eyes glowing with mirth. "Play cards with a professional? I would be demolished."

"You do not know that. We could find out."

She narrowed her gaze. "Ah. You would enjoy beating me."

He had to guard his thoughts from such an image. "I would take the gamble."

She smoothed her glorious hair. "I will leave you to wonder if I might win. What else can you do, Allan?"

He eyed her. "Do?"

"I believe you possess other skills. Oxford surely must have set you on your way. These last several years have perhaps taken you from your true path."

She demurely drank her brandy. He drained his glass.

"That, like me," she continued airily, "you were caught up in circumstances that forced your hand. I ran away, so I suppose you did, also. I know I have no right to—"

"No, you do not," he quickly stated, snatching her glass and placing both on a table. "I ran away before I murdered someone."

"Oh, I cannot credit that, Allan. You are not a

killer."

"Damn it," he raged, "would you cease—" Then Allan felt so angry, so bitterly thwarted, so goddamned miserable, he pulled the chit into his arms and soundly kissed her sassy mouth.

Completely caught by surprise, for a split second Marissa became highly offended, ready to smack him in the nose, then everything stopped. Her heartbeat, her common sense, all social rules drummed into her since infancy, halted. Marissa swam out into unknown waters and, exhilarated, breathed in Allan Rutledge like an elusive, tantalizing vapor. Her arms went around his shoulders of their own volition. She teetered on the edge of a swoon, caressed the back of his neck, and pulled a tuft of his hair, just to get the feel of him.

He must weigh ten stone, and it all fell on her like a heap of pillows. Marissa realized she had become trapped under Allan on the less than roomy settee. This would not do! She gave him a little push.

He sprang to his feet, startling both of them. "I did not plan that," he explained.

"All the better," Marissa replied, sitting up.

He glared at her.

She straightened the silk gown. "I said things you did not care to hear. So, you shut me up in a very male way."

Allan bristled with frustration, and Marissa had never been so entertained. He took her arm and lifted her to her feet. Stared into her eyes and demanded, "Who are you? Where do you come from?"

"Ewell, Surrey."

"Who are your people?"

She jerked away. "Do not be a brute and heave all

your doubts my direction. You liked kissing me, and I liked it, too. But if you try it again in such a boorish manner, without my consent, I will strike you with the nearest heavy object. As to my family connections, I assure you they are most reputable. Excepting my father has lost his reason, infected with treasure fever. I have little money and no powerful friends, but I will function quite well in London, thank you. I am a capable woman. So there."

"How do you know so much?" he mumbled.

"What kinds of brainless ladies have you known?"

"The wrong kind. Certainly, no one like you, with your lofty opinions."

"Then allow me to be a better example." Her perception changed. "Unless you mean I am a mess."

A tap at the door, and Murray entered. "Dinner," he intoned.

"Many thanks, Murray," Allan replied. He stood and offered his arm.

Marissa, in her fine silk gown, recently kissed and vigorously debated by Allan, took it and floated from the room.

Allan fancied himself to be seldom out of control, but this woman cracked his defenses like an eggshell. Unpredictable females disturbed him. Many women were easy to figure out, all behaving in the same patterns, but not Marissa.

He escorted her to the dining room, a relatively cozy space despite its size, and held her chair. She sat, and once again, he caught her scent, something like lilacs. Allan sat at the head, and Murray entered, bearing a tureen. At the sideboard, he ladled out soup and brought bowls to the table—creamy mushroom—then he poured

Allan's favorite white wine. Marissa dipped her spoon and ate hungrily. When had he ever seen a woman eat with real enjoyment?

Allan ate and watched her. She needed watching.

"Oh, Murray," she crooned. "This is delicious."

Murray nodded impassively but blushed, his cheeks rosy. They finished, and the man collected bowls.

She sipped the wine. "And the white Burgundy," she praised. "A fine choice."

Allan became certain she had changed into a sorceress. Murray would melt onto the floor like candle wax. His whole life would be blotted, Allan mourned; he never should have gotten her that hack. Should have walked away. She might be the worst decision so far in his frayed life. She eagerly awaited the next course, her hazel eyes bright, and Murray did not fail. In he marched with two plates, each containing a row of shrimp and a line of horseradish sauce.

Marissa regarded this, dipped an edge in the sauce, and ate one. "My," she said cheerfully, "rather hot," and ate the rest.

Allan stuffed in his, ignoring the burn. "I like it," he said. "I like hot things." Impulsively, he waggled his brows.

"I imagine you do," she replied.

Murray poured more wine, a red this time, and removed dishes.

She finished the Burgundy and gazed at Allan. "I forgot to ask if you are married," she murmured.

"Careless of you. I am not, nor have I ever considered it."

"Never for a moment?" she queried. "Never pictured the faces of your children or how it would be to have a wife?"

"What do I need with a wife!" he exclaimed.

Marissa sat back, giving him a speaking look. "She would like you all the time, even when you were cross and cantankerous. Which you rather are."

He gathered himself to scald her tiny ears, but Murray entered, bearing the main course.

"Oh," Marissa cried, "what a splendid bird. Such a fine color, difficult to achieve."

Allan wanted to slide from the room before he became sullied with sweetness.

Murray sliced and filled their plates. Damnable Marissa talked about lemon chicken, whatever the hell that might be. Murray's big feet might leave the floor, he looked so delighted. Allan sighed. Two days and it would be over. He could return to his dismal life, and— but no! The truth of it forcefully washed over him. Eban and Cordelia, dead and gone! Marissa had distracted him from the stupendous event.

Immediately, his mood lightened, and he cut into his chicken. Marissa discussed the virtues of various peas with an attentive Murray. Allan felt like he had landed in the wrong house.

Excited by it all, Marissa felt about to foam over like ale. The fine meal had been prepared by Murray, and she had not had to lift a hand. The roasted fowl, the special wines, both were table luxuries she had recently done without, and she reveled in them.

Allan ate in a vigilant manner, mostly keeping his gaze on her. Marissa imagined him in some cavernous gambling hell, that sharp concentration on the other players, all dangerous, bad men. He would intimidate them with his ferocious glances. It made her heart flutter to think of his manly powers. None of his ire was directed at her, or she would wither into a crone.

However, he had proved to be a rascal on the settee. It seemed to her a wonder they had not rolled into the fireplace. She had to suppress a laugh and could not think what might happen next.

Dessert consisted of a small, round sponge cake covered with sugared, sliced strawberries. "Oh, Murray," she breathed. "I do love fresh berries."

The man smiled broadly, revealing a set of very white teeth. Marissa felt a great fondness for the enormous man.

"I have never had a better meal. Thank you."

Murray left the room. Allan considered her, his glance wary.

"Did you not think so, Allan?" she asked.

"Indeed," he admitted.

Really, he needed a poke. "I know how much effort it takes to put a fine meal like this on the table. Piping hot, well-seasoned, and all the rest. The meat done to a turn. You should try it, Allan. Murray is very talented."

"I am aware of this. I have no skill in the kitchen. Likely, I could not properly heat water. I know Murray to be a prize. Without him, I would have starved and fallen into rags long ago."

She ate her berries one by one. "Fresh strawberries are like eating Spring."

"Hmmm," Allan remarked.

Marissa watched him enjoy his food. Such a fine-looking man, she mused. She licked sweet juices from her spoon, comfortably full, the wonderful dinner over.

As Allan finished, the valet/cook returned. "A superb meal, Murray," he praised the man.

Marissa beamed, gratified to hear this.

"Thank you, sir. Coffee in the drawing room?"

"That would be grand. Shall we, Marissa?"

"Yes, coffee will be perfect. Thank you again, Murray."

His expression pleased, Murray retreated. Allan offered his arm, and they strolled from the lovely room. Gosh, what else might happen? Her heart thumped. Allan Rutledge, captivatingly hazardous and possibly deceitful, may be setting her up for some alarming consequence. Marissa could not wait to find out what it might be, confident that, if necessary, she would have no trouble handling this intriguing man.

Chapter Three

His belly full, Allan now regarded the troublesome woman with a clear head. How much did he have to tell her of his affairs? The woman was constantly curious, so he must decide in time to head her off. He did not like to divulge his plans, secrets, or whatever occupied his mind.

"Why did you kiss me?" she naïvely asked, throwing him off balance.

"The usual reasons a man kisses a woman. And besides," he confessed, "I became irritated. You ask a lot of questions, and I am unused to that, um, imposition."

Undaunted, she nodded knowingly. "Of course, it would seem an intrusion, since you have no one to converse with. This, I have found, is the problem with solitude. It becomes very easy to shut everything up, think you are doing well, then someone speaks and throws you into a tremor."

"I do not have tremors," he asserted.

She folded her hands primly. "I certainly did. I had not a soul to confide my thoughts and fears to. This, I found, posed a great impediment. One lacks another point of view and can spin in circles."

"Does one?" he said, humoring her.

"Yes. We are a social people. We need friends and, at best, a close companion. I had so much housework, I could no longer spare the time to attend assemblies and occasional parties. My clothes began to wear out. My hands—" She gazed sadly at them.

Allan, struck with an avalanche of sympathy that threatened to inundate him, steadfastly fought his way out of it.

Marissa raised her pert chin. "But I must not complain. I kept it all going, but now I am done. I mean to find, or rather, to make, a better life. I will not dwell on what I have lost, my home, my security, my proper place. The future is ahead of me."

He thought of dragging his past and his burning fury behind him all this time. Allan would do the same, if he could, move on, forget his wrath. What good had it served? He, too, had "kept it going," but like Marissa, he too, was done, both of his betrayers dead.

"Your labors have not diminished you, Marissa. They have made you strong. And you are young, beautiful, and smart, so life will be good to you."

"Oh," she breathed, "do you actually think so?"

"Yes, I do."

Murray entered with the coffee tray and placed it on a low table nearby. "Thank you, Murray," Allan said. "Your efforts are most appreciated."

Visibly pleased, Murray murmured, "Thank you, sir," and departed. Marissa poured two cups and handed him one.

Allan dropped in a lump of sugar, as did she, and they stirred. He allowed maybe he had become stronger, too. Certainly, he had run a gauntlet of torment, but that would change. Allan let himself expand into the new reality, and a modicum of ease crept into his shoulders.

"So," she unexpectedly asked, "what is ahead for you, Allan?"

More of her intrusive questions. He tried to be civilized and better tempered. "With my guardian in Hades, his despicable wife with him, I will go home."

"Mercy," she said, bending toward him. "You disliked them both?"

Allan tasted bile. "With my very soul."

She paused thoughtfully. "He hurt you?"

He shook his head, trying to shake off the anger. "Not physically."

"Tell me what he did," she urged. "It might relieve your mind to speak of it."

Allan prepared a dismissive remark, then let it pass. Where to begin? Go back. "My father died; I had just reached seventeen. Old Eban Newton, my father's cousin, a man in ill health, got appointed my guardian by the court until I reached my majority.

"Heavily involved at Oxford, I kept on with my studies, trusting the man would keep a grip on things. At the end of my final term, I went home, eager to take my place. There, I discovered Eban had married a woman much younger than himself, of low standing, who had a palpable interest in money. I sensed she had a plan to acquire it. His health had deteriorated, and I quickly gauged the woman waited for his eventual death, to come into his money. It soon became evident that she did not like me. Eban, I found, had become remote, and we seldom spoke."

Allan paused until he could resume. "I had not been on the premises for a sennight, when he summoned me to his presence and ordered me from the house."

"Ohhhh," Marissa cried.

This fueled Allan's energy to tell it all. "I demanded a reason; I was now one and twenty, they were in my house and on my land. Everything constituted my rightful inheritance. Finally, when compelled by me, Eban revealed his wife, Cordelia, had accused me of molesting her. In short, attempted rape. I quickly became outraged, and a quarrel ensued. I demanded she face me with her accusations, but she would not. Eban feigned weakness and poor health, crying I had become wicked and depraved, and he could do nothing."

Marissa put her small hand on his arm. Allan gazed into her face and told her everything.

"I loaded a pistol and meant to kill her. Or him. Or both. I got all the way to his door and heard them laughing. They were a pair of vampires, but murder would be insane. I would not go to prison for the likes of them and left the house before I did anything regrettable. That happened three years ago."

Allan sat back, quite relieved, just as Marissa had predicted. "A visit to my solicitor told my fate. My father's will was sound; everything came to me. However, Eban's man had invoked a legal statute stating an inheritance could be delayed by the appointed guardian if the heir displayed 'grave immoral conduct.' And it could last indefinitely, until I reformed or some goddamn thing. Pardon me. They would continue to live in my house, on my land. I would receive a pittance of the estate income, which I never trusted as accurate, and soon I found it not enough to live on."

"Such injustice, Allan," Marissa bemoaned. "How unbearable for you."

Her understanding thrilled him. "Hunh. I got along."

"I would have cried myself sick. I think you are very brave."

Allan wanted to put his head in her lap and be

comforted.

Marissa's heart went out to him. She had lost her home through her father's fixation, but Allan had been outright cheated. He had heard them laughing but turned away from violence. What fortitude! She longed to soothe him for, well, everything. The thought of holding him and stroking his pretty, dark hair became so actual, she nearly reached out to do so.

Allan was heavily enticing. Marissa longed to get nearer and find out everything he knew. They had been in each other's company for all this long day. Not only highly unusual behavior, but strictly forbidden, she might as well admit. She wondered if her father had realized she had gone. Likely, when he got no dinner.

Not to mention the dastardly duke and his presumptions. Certain that he could dole out his dirty coins, crook a finger, and she would be his to drag around. Why did he want an unwilling bride who despised him? Love? No. He had become obsessed, too.

When the dolt had first begun to pursue her after the new year, Marissa had ignored him. This had not gone over well. Unaccustomed to being shunted aside, the duke doubled his efforts and began a feverish, entirely one-sided courtship. She evaded and avoided, but he had offered Father hard cash, and as it turned out, the decision had never been in her hands.

Marissa regarded those long legs. If he had been Allan Rutledge—

"So, they are dead," he went on, "killed in a carriage accident, of all things. Tomorrow, I must see my solicitor, speak with him, then go down to Kent, and my home."

Shocking! He would leave her? The idea almost

stopped her heart, but she said, "Oh. I will go about my business. Find a suitable place to stay until Monday. See a bit of the town."

Allan glanced sideways toward her. "Come with me. If the weather continues fine, it is a nice ride."

She felt a blush begin and bit her lower lip. "I would not wish to be in your way."

"You would not be in my way, Marissa; we would be together. Besides, the thought of you wandering around London alone gives me palpitations."

"I must begin sometime," Marissa insisted.

"When your aunt returns will be soon enough. She will have suitable provisions. Therefore."

"Provisions?"

He waved a hand. "Trappings of respectability suitable for a young lady. A proper household, a maid, and so on."

She frowned. "And a cat that howls."

"A bonus. It will love you and purr." His gaze became penetrating. "Does not everyone love you, Marissa?"

"Not so I have noticed."

"What about that enamored duke? Which one is he, by the by?"

"Are there so few?"

"God, no, they must grow on bushes. Which of them became enraptured by your abundant attractions?"

"Have I attractions, Allan?" she inquired. "Name them, please."

"Let me think." He paused and scratched his chin. He regarded the shine on his boots.

Marissa poured a second cup, added a sugar cube, and watched it dissolve. "Well! I am sorry I asked."

"I am considering. You have too many to list."

"Bosh," she huffed. "That saves you from saying I have none."

He rose. "Let us have another brandy."

She simmered with annoyance. He returned with two glasses. Marissa took one but did not glance his way.

Allan took his seat. "It is not good to fish for praise, girl."

"How else should I get any?" she snapped. "I would wager you are stingy with compliments. You do not like women."

"Who said so?" he demanded.

"You croaked out, 'vurry prutty,' when you saw this wonderful gown, like it hurt your tongue to say it. And you only kissed me to close my mouth."

"You opened your mouth."

"I did not!"

"Yes, you did. You are as ripe as a peach, you minx, and twice as juicy. You may be, no, you are, the most enchanting woman I have ever encountered. You bubble with life, have a brain in your head, captivating attributes, skin like a rose petal, and I would like to kiss and bite you all over until you shout."

Marissa sat there, stunned.

"Therefore, do not be asking me to enumerate your womanly assets. Or I may become lured away and act on my impulses. You should go to bed. There is a lock on your door. Use it."

She loved this game. "I am not afraid of you, Mister Big, Bad Wolf."

"You should be. I am a false grandmama to little girls like you."

"Oh, how superior."

"I have sharp teeth," he warned, with a vicious glare.

Marissa giggled.

Damnation. So daft, the girl could not take him seriously. He would scare her off. Allan moved closer and aimed to threaten.

"Do you not perceive we are alone here?" he growled. "Or what a man like me could do to wreck your prospects?"

"What kind of man are you?" she asked, her hazel eyes wide.

He grimaced. "One who has seen the underside of life."

"Oh? What does it look like? Is everyone upside down?"

"Actually, yes. And I joined them in their depravity."

She blinked. "Depravity?"

"Blast it, Marissa, do not these terms define themselves?"

"Words do not mean; people mean. You say these ominous things, Allan, but they lack conviction. I am aware you would like to be rid of me, and tomorrow I will go. In the meantime, I think I would have to twist your arm to share another of those impressive kisses. Unless you get sufficiently mad again."

Allan went on, undefeated. "You are playing with hot coals, girl. I hope you indulged in none of this behavior with that duke."

"Certainly not. I thought him revolting. However, you are very attractive, Allan, and I would like to learn a little more about—"

He seized her in his arms. "I could overwhelm you in five seconds."

She gazed into his eyes. "Maybe only three."

Allan laughed, hugged her, and moved away. "I am definitely not leaving you on your own, Marissa. You are a danger to the male population."

"Ah, but not to you, I see." She slumped into the cushions. "My future looks drab. No one will want a person who has no experience of the world, stuck in the country, cut off from any meaningful knowledge."

"You may place a notice in the *Times*," he suggested. " 'Lady with no experience desires same with congenial partner. A man is preferred.' "

She laughed prettily. "Would someone answer, do you think?"

"In droves. Even if you were homely."

"They would have no way to know that. I might be an imbecile and have a bump on the end of my nose."

"Such are the hazards of faceless romance."

"Like meeting someone at a masked ball," she dreamily said.

Marissa must have some kind of past. "Have you ever been to a masquerade?" he inquired.

"Sadly, no. The entertainments in Ewell were not so gaudy. It always sounded like great fun."

"Fun," he grumbled.

"You have had some of that, have you not, Allan? I would guess you went to such a ball, all dressed up like a pirate."

He eyed her. "Eh? Why a pirate?"

"It suits you. You are an adventurer at heart. You went from the towers of Oxford to basements full of treacherous card sharks."

"Cardsharps," Allan corrected.

"Yes. You are bold and brave and not above fleecing

the rogues with your intelligence. A fine pirate, there."

"I never played cards in basements," he objected. "I did not sink that low."

"Never mind. It must have felt like it. No wonder you got so furious at yourself."

He leaned away. "Whaaat?"

"For being there! You are a gentleman. Before your father died, you must have been carried about on a bolster. You knew your place and hated to leave it. And I cannot believe you gave that man's wife so much as a furtive squeeze. It is not in your character to behave so."

Allan meant to discourage her, sort of, and became menacing. "I might give you a few squeezes, Miss Know-It-All. So, take heed."

"That would be different. We are friends, you said so."

And Marissa looked so soft, so comforting, so willing, Allan gathered her up and kissed her again.

She fell from a high place into feathers. Marissa sank into Allan's arms and returned every nuance of the beguiling kiss, the closeness, the being one with him for the moment. She tried to catch every sensation, like capturing the wind, but he slipped away even as she held him.

"Listen," he began. Then to her joy, Allan kissed her some more. She put her arms around his neck and breathed him in, tasted him, and relished the flavors. This went on for so long, she lost her bearings and reality became distorted.

"Marissa," he whispered, from some place far away.

She opened her eyes. "Yes? Yes?"

"How much do you know about sex?"

She hid her surprise.

"About intimacy between a man and a woman," he went on, his expression cautious.

"The rudiments," she murmured.

He leaned away and began to laugh.

"There is nothing humorous about it, Allan," she said, insulted. "Woman are kept sealed in a jar, then are supposed to know all about everything? It is grossly unfair, and I mentioned I had no one to talk to after my mother went. I have read a few things, but beyond the fundamentals, I have had scant opportunity to increase my—"

"Then do not give away kisses so lightly," he scolded.

Marissa pushed him off and stood. "That is all you know, Allan. I am tired now and will seek my bed. Thank you for absolutely everything. Tomorrow, I will be out of your hair, and the next man who kisses me will find I have some knowledge to go by. Good night."

She marched out, her back straight. Let him think that over. She climbed the stairs, still glowing from his attentions. She had gotten her squeeze and then some from the grudging man. And without a doubt, Marissa had loved all of it.

Allan sat there as the fire died. Blast the girl, meandering into his life like this. Stirring up old grievances and failures. So he had a few shortcomings! Such female impertinence. How did she think she knew him after one day?

But…

The things she said had struck him squarely in his gut. He had no one to talk to, either. Had steeped in his own juices for so long, he had forgotten himself. Turned out unjustly, he had buried his principled feelings under the concrete of his wrath. Marissa opened doors he had forgotten, and it all flooded in like water, who he had become and who he had meant to be.

He must not kiss her again. Bloody hell. Where would that get him? He had been locked up like a tomb, and she could help him climb out. Hungry, he would consume her, but he must not. Keep it easy, keep it casual.

What a sweetheart, though, he admitted. Fresh and untouched. Beautiful, female, giving, and fragrant. Maybe his turmoil had ended, and by some twist of fate, Marissa had come along to redeem him. He found this startling to consider. Had everything come around in his favor, all in this busy day? Could it be possible?

He turned down the lamps and, in the darkness, made his way up the stairs. Marissa would sleep in his borrowed house, a lady not his own. Practically a stranger, she had moved his life over. Meeting her seemed the most significant thing that could have happened. Allan felt a great weight had moved off his soul. He went to his room, his barren existence quite suddenly full of promise.

****

Saturday

Marissa woke with the light, long her habit. She opened her eyes to view an ornate ceiling decorated with a painted group of cherubs. They all looked down at her with amused reproach as if she had been naughty. She luxuriated in the soft bed and stretched all over. Then she hopped out and carefully remade the bed, smoothing the linens and fluffing up the pillows.

She had scarcely wrinkled anything; no one would know. Mercy, this intrusion on top of wearing someone's glorious dress. She had slept in her chemise in case she had to rise in a hurry. Marissa used the last of the water in the pitcher to bathe her face, dressed in her familiar garments, and brushed out her hair. All this in something of a tizzy. She piled it all up again with the aid of her pins and faced the glass.

She had kissed Allan a number of times. Now what would he think? She must rush off after, hopefully, a good breakfast, to the Bank of England, wherever it was located. Would her five shillings sixpence be enough for a hackney?

Marissa felt the freezing clutch of uncertainty. The city stretched out around her for miles and miles. She had no idea where she stood in its vastness. In Ewell, she could walk from one end of the town to another and back again and not be tired. She almost sat down on the bed to think but did not want to crease it. Instead, she paced around.

Buck up, he had said. Thinking of everything else he had said gave her a tremble. She had left him last night somewhat irritated; she would make that up. Allan continued to be a nice man, despite his suit of spiky armor.

Apprehensive, she unlocked the door and left the room, the house silent. Had she been abandoned, to be sold to those Egyptians? But small noises reached her. She smelled toast and coffee, ran down the stairs and on to a breakfast room painted a cool lemon yellow. It made the entire room radiant with sunlight.

Allan stood by a cherry sideboard, a plate in his hand, looking like a prince.

"Good morning, Allan."

"Good morning. Did you rest well?"

"I did, thank you."

He handed her a plate.

"Did you?" she asked.

"Eventually." He paused. "I do not sleep well."

"What constitutes well?" Marissa asked, choosing a sausage and whipped eggs. She added a slice of toast. "Do you have bad dreams? Not sleep long enough, or not at all?"

"Uh—"

She took a chair at the table, and Allan sat at the head. Murray came into the room with a silver coffeepot.

"Good morning, Murray."

Big smile. "Good morning, Miss Barrington."

He poured coffee and departed. How could she help Allan?

"Perhaps you have dreams and wake. For a time, I had a worrying dream," she related. "It spoiled my rest."

Allan lifted a forkful of eggs and looked wary.

"I dreamed I had lost my reticule, which contained all my information, everything about me. My identity, you see, was missing. I searched everywhere, retraced my steps, all the while becoming more and more upset. Then I would wake up. This went on until I had had enough of it." She ate a bite of the delicious eggs. "So, I firmly decided not to have it anymore." Marissa put plum jam on her toast, bit in, and chewed.

"Well?" Allan asked. "Did that work?"

She swallowed. "Yes, it did. I realized I was safely me, reticule or no."

He appeared baffled.

"I will not be plagued by bad thoughts I myself have invented," she explained. "I think you will sleep, Allan, when you are no longer unhappy."

Allan would like to spank her for her infernal, intrusive, ill-mannered, girlish pomposity. However, it all sounded true. She had, in some imperceptible way, captivated his mind. Marissa reduced his resistance to putty and erased his various clumps of anger.

She dropped her toast to her plate. "Oh, dear. I have said too much."

"Oh?" he snarled.

"You have that kill-her-now look."

The girl was definitely loopy. What he wanted to do with her had nothing to do with murder. Allan wanted to devour her and be a better man.

"Be that as it may," he pronounced, "what say we travel first to see my solicitor, then journey on to Kent?"

She stopped moving. He heard her breathe. "Together? All that way?"

"I cannot leave you here. Besides, do you not want to see the world? Or about sixteen miles of it? We will have some of that fun you mentioned. I am as dry as gin without it."

"I would go," she whispered.

"Therefore. We will leave in one half hour."

"I will be ready," she said, finished her coffee, excused herself, and left the table.

Allan immediately missed her. Everything she said gave him a jolt. He had been living in a box. No one had said anything insightful to him in an age. Damn hard to think things out alone. But Marissa had, while peeling those vegetables.

Very well, he had been digging a ditch for himself for three years. Full of self-pity, one might say. That one being Marissa.

Murray kindly gave him fresh coffee.

"The girl is something, eh, Murray?"

He nodded solemnly. "A rare one, sir."

"I am off to the country after seeing Stubbins. We should be back tomorrow evening, I reckon."

Murray appeared doubtful.

Allan waved a hand. "I will make no mischief, be assured. Marissa is an upright girl. On Monday, she goes to the care of her aunt, and that will be the end of it."

"Yes, sir," Murray said, as he left. But the man did not sound convinced.

****

Marissa rearranged her things in the valise. She ought to change into the carriage dress, but it would be a bother. She fitted it in and went to the dressing room for her other clothing. There hung the lovely, rose silk gown. She took her old things and, with a twinge, left the beautiful silk garments behind. She packed, suffered an immense longing, and went back to again see the rose dress. So perfect, but no, she admonished, loving the rich, supple fabric. You cannot have it. She pinned on her hat and pushed at the white flower.

The last years of worry and painful deprivation overwhelmed her better sense, and hurrying, she took the lovely gown and gently folded it into the valise. When she had her money, she would pay a generous amount to whomever it belonged and buy it. This salved her conscience somewhat. She had to have it. To wear for Allan. To be pretty and feel special. She snapped the valise closed and felt condemned.

Marissa took the garment out again and carefully hung it in the dressing room. "I will have another someday, even lovelier than this," she said to herself, closed the valise, and left the room.

She flew down the stairs, lugging the valise, but Allan had not yet arrived. Murray, on duty in the foyer, had his large hands folded before him, his expression patient.

"Murray, thank you for being so kind to me and taking extra trouble."

He nodded. "A pleasure to serve you, Miss Barrington."

She had time to ask questions. "Have you been with Allan long?"

"Over two years now. I can readily say he is a good man, a decent man, if that is a question."

"He seems so to me and has been most helpful. Such a time, would you not say? Everything is going to change for all of us," she asserted.

"Yes, ma'am. I know it is."

Allan came down the stairs with his portmanteau. Marissa's heart beat faster. His fine clothes, his regal bearing.

"Murray," he said, "we are off. The carriage has arrived?"

"Yes, sir, it awaits. Griggs related—"

The doorbell whirred and chimed. Murray crossed to it and opened it to a small man, who appeared perturbed. Marissa leaned past Murray to clearly see his face, gasped, stepped back, and flattened herself to the wall.

"Yes?" Murray inquired.

The short, rather plump man cleared his throat. "I would speak with your master, if you please."

Allan stepped forward. "I am he. State your business."

The man drew himself up and presented a letter.

"Important correspondence, sir."

Allan took it, unfolded the heavy paper, and read. "Do come in, my man," he cordially invited.

"Nay, I will not."

"I must insist. Murray, help this fellow inside."

Murray reached out and lifted the man bodily as he shrieked and placed him down on the floor. The front door closed.

"I will not be treated so!" he cried, straightening his coat. "I personally represent the Duke of Ludlow and am here at His Grace's lawful bidding."

"Is that a fact?" Allan countered. He waved the paper. "This missive is not directed to me. It is an open document."

"No matter! I tracked you both here. Where is the lady?"

Allan frowned mightily, plotting strategy. "I assume you refer to my fiancée?"

"No, indeed I do not. I refer only to Miss Barrington. I demand—" He spotted her. "There you are, miss! I am come to bring you home."

Marissa moved away from the wall. "Balderdash, Shaw. I am not going back. I have no interest whatsoever in His Grace and have repeatedly told him so. It is undignified on the part of both of you to hie after me in this manner."

Shaw appeared uninterested. "The contracts have been signed," he righteously stated. "The agreement is binding. I am here to fetch you, with orders to take every effort necessary. You are in danger of violating the law if you do not comply."

"Ah, the law," Allan repeated, pulling his chin. "A serious matter, indeed. Murray, show the gentleman into the drawing room. I will be along. Remember to put away the chess set."

"This way, sir," Murray intoned, gesturing to the door. Shaw, with a triumphant glance, followed him, his pointy nose in the air.

So, she had told the truth. "Let us go, Marissa," Allan directed, taking the baggage.

No sound from the drawing room. They hurried out the door and to a carriage. The groom quickly lashed their luggage aboard. Marissa watched the house for trouble but saw nothing amiss.

Allan spoke to the coachman. "To Oxford and New Bond, Griggs."

"Aye, sir."

Allan swung in, closed the door, and off they went. Marissa breathed a long sigh of relief. She regarded him, sitting close to her. His *fiancée*, Allan had said. Her spirits went glimmering. She had hoped—never mind, never mind. It had been too amazing to last. He had someone he loved. Allan had no obligation to tell her anything about it. She sat back, resigned. Thank heaven she did not take that lovely silk gown.

With the arrival of Shaw, Allan definitely would not let Marissa out of his sight. The gall of this bastard Ludlow, sending his man to "fetch" her, like a sack of grain. He gazed at her, pretty in a modest sage-green gown of soft material. Little brown half boots on her feet. The tapestry reticule, the hat with the drooping flower.

"What did the letter say?" she asked.

He handed it to her.

She unfolded it and read. "What! Ten thousand pounds?"

"The villain duke aims to have you back. You are

not going. Murray will keep his lackey occupied. He cannot know where we have gone."

"Shaw tracked us, he said. Can it be?"

"Easily done, my girl. You would be memorable in Ewell. We both boarded the mail coach and likely attracted attention in the process. It headed to the Star Inn, and the hack we chose likely favors that location. For a ha'penny, he would tell brother Shaw everywhere we visited."

"Ohhhh," she grumbled.

It riled him. "Shaw set out from Ewell with that prepared letter to buy you back from me."

"From you?"

"Since I have you," he teased. "All yesterday and all last night."

She pensively handed back the letter. "So much money. What a dunce Ludlow is. What can he be thinking?"

Allan read a passage aloud. " 'Return Miss Marissa Barrington to me, alive, well, and untouched, and the sum of ten thousand pounds will be yours,' et cetera and so forth. The alive part covers if you had been kidnapped, I suppose."

Annoyed, she said, "It is all a falsehood. He just wants me to come to heel. No sensible person would pay such an amount, or any amount, for someone who loathes them." She studied him. "Would you pay for the return of your fiancée? The one you mentioned?"

He shrugged. "I just said that. To save your reputation."

"From whom?"

"From the world! It would mitigate gossip, if we were runaway lovers. Even the ton would accept that. Ill-fated sweethearts, a hasty pursuit, and a vengeful duke—the whole thing would have them by the ears."

"That group is the least of my worries. Well. We have left Shaw to Murray's tender mercies." She looked out the window. "Oh, we are stopping?"

"Stubbins, my solicitor, is on this street. You wait here, Marissa, in safety."

Will, the groom, got the door, and Allan stepped down to the busy sidewalk. The girl looked all directions with delight, hurrying people everywhere. He entered a heavy, paneled door. It closed with a clunk, and abruptly, the room became quiet. A clerk rose from his desk.

"My lord, good day."

"Greene. Is the man in?"

"He is, sir. Allow me to announce you." He strode down a hall and immediately returned. "Come through, my lord."

He headed that way. At the first open door, Allan sauntered in. Stubbins dropped a folder, jumped to his feet, and strode toward him. They shook hands.

"Allan, old man. You spoke to Murray?"

"I did. He told me everything."

The tall, wiry man nodded, making his longish dark hair fall forward. "Take a seat, please." He moved to sit behind his cluttered desk as they did so.

"Well, Allan, just the most astonishing news, eh? Eban and Cordelia met a sad end."

"I am all broken up, Stubbins," he said with a smile.

"Ah, so were they," the man cheerfully related. "But that aside, the entirety of the estate is now in your hands. I have already seen to transfers of titles, all right and legal, just as it should have been years ago."

Allan had to ask. "It is all over? My supposed moral

corruption?"

Stubbins rooted in his papers and handed over a letter. "After the funeral, I chanced to find this at the Hall."

Allan took it. A short note, in Eban's shaky hand.

February 10, 1815
Allan. I have done you a great injury. Cordelia has confessed her treachery. You were innocent of the despicable accusation, and I beg your forgiveness. I have not long in the world and this falsehood has troubled me severely, but I could not find you to say so, or make it right.
Eban Newton

What the hell, written more than two years ago? He folded the paper and put it in his pocket.

"You are cleared of any wrongdoing, Allan," Stubbins said with glee. "You can go home."

"Yes, I am headed that way. My accounts are straight?"

"Every debt has been paid. The bank has been informed, papers, drafts, and so on will arrive every fortnight. You are on your way, my lord."

The men stood.

"Stubbins, I am grateful for everything, all this time."

"It is a great satisfaction to me to see it all come around as it should. Keep in touch. I will send further documents along to the Hall as soon as they are complete."

Allan considered the situation. He needed to make a statement. "Stubbins, I need a favor."

"Anything, Allan."

Allan took a sheet of paper and began to write. "I want this placed prominently in Sunday's Times. Just as it reads."

Stubbins took it. "Very well. Anything else?"

"Not yet, my friend. Not yet, but as you said, I am on my way. See you soon."

Allan left the office for the busy street and the waiting carriage.

Chapter Four

They drove away, Marissa jubilant. Oxford Street, surely the busiest and most colorful location in London, had an array of interesting shops and stands. More modishly dressed people had passed by the carriage than she had ever seen. The air smelled of oily, roasted nuts, something sugary, and ground coffee. Cut flowers of all sorts were loudly offered for sale by lads bearing buckets of water. The carriage rolled on, and the street seemed to have no end.

"I would imagine," Allan drawled, "that you would have liked to visit the fine shops."

"Oh, it would be enough to stand on a corner and observe the people. That would be interesting in the extreme."

She could not see enough of it all at once. Then the crowds began to thin, the shops and businesses became housing, and gradually, they left the city and all its activity behind. Marissa sat back. Though not yet noon, the day had been eventful.

Allan relaxed in the other seat, his long legs stretched out to one side, so as not to crowd her. Murray had declared Allan to be *a good man, a decent man.* How sweet of him. He had no call to reassure her, but he had.

"I liked Murray very much, Allan."

"He liked you."

"What do you suppose he did with Shaw?"

"Delayed him, allowing us to leave. The fellow would have hung on to you like a terrier with a ferret. Murray will set him loose in an hour or two. No harm done."

"Shaw will be livid," she breathed. "He is the duke's faithful donkey and used to watch me every day."

Allan grimaced. "Oh, say not."

Marissa nodded. "He settled himself outside, pretending to observe the workers, but if I left the house to go into Ewell, he followed at a little distance. I confronted him about this, but he just smirked like a goat and would not go away."

"Well, he must now return to Ewell to be flogged by His Grace," Allan happily remarked, "having failed his mission."

"Just a dogsbody."

"Ha! Where did you hear such a word?"

"It is a Royal Navy term for someone who only does menial, boring tasks. I remember everything I read, as I said."

"Recite something."

"Of what sort?"

"How are you with poetry? Give me a favorite."

The man meant to challenge her! What crust. "It is rather long."

He waved a careless hand. Marissa began.

"All the words that go unsaid
Can grow a garden
In your head,
To form a poem
Or a lofty tome,
Make a picture,
Loosen every stricture,

Or, lacking this vital toil,
Spoil and rot
Into a bitter knot.
Speak, speak,
Is the game,
To give the least of things
A name."

A silence fell as Allan stared at her. Marissa blushed hotly, embarrassed. Her little scratching; less than nothing. She should not have—

Allan leaned forward, his hands on his knees. "Most unusual. I have some knowledge of poetry, but never— whose work is that?"

"Only just a scrawl," she said, humbled.

He paused. "Noooo; is it yours?"

"Writing is like having someone to speak to," Marissa urgently replied. "I had no one, so I wrote, and it became a comfort, an outlet. Like a letter to a friend, telling them my thoughts. However, I had no correspondent."

Marissa shrank into the corner of the seat. How could she face him? Allan must think her a rural fool.

Allan, freshly astounded by this girl, knew her mind teemed with unfamiliar things. At Oxford, he had seen clever friends struggle to get a meaningful line down on paper, but Marissa just rolled it out like pastry.

"I am impressed, Marissa. It is no small thing to successfully express your thoughts. Just to have access to them defeats many."

She would not look at him, the timid creature.

"I am honored you revealed your talent. Believe me, I thought it a fine bit of verse and in a form such as I have not heard before. Uh, have you written more?"

She dared to raise her eyes. "Do not mock me, Allan."

"I am not! I mean what I say. I would be proud to claim it as my own. I hear echoes of Blake and Thomas Gray. But you are a modern person, and I note a change in language and its usage. Did you have a tutor?"

She smoothed her gown. "I had a knowledgeable governess until Mother died, Miss Grisham. We did a lot of reading together as I got older. Then Father let her go; he needed her salary. I wept, beyond unhappy to lose her."

"Oh, the losses, eh?" Allan bemoaned. "They haunt us."

"Whom did you lose?"

"Everyone." He gazed out the window. "Soon we will reach a well-known coaching inn and have some luncheon. What say you?"

"That would be lovely."

Allan sat back. Small wonder the blasted duke went to great lengths to have her. A polished diamond had been hidden away in Ewell, but Ludlow had found her, the swine. He well remembered the man's cold visage, his tight grin barely disguising a ruthless nature. His face had been shadowed in the plush surroundings of the Nightingale, but Allan had seen him for a scoundrel, had out-maneuvered him at vingt-et-un, and walked away with his money.

Palpable hatred had followed him until Allan left the club. He had never wanted to see the man again. Unexpected to encounter him in this way. Just the thought of him mauling Marissa, the delicate child, tore his heart.

Allan steeled himself. The Duke of Ludlow would

never have her, no matter what it took. In these circumstances, Marissa needed his care. Yes. She practically belonged to him. Short term. For the interim. How long could he make it last?

The carriage pulled into the Crescent Inn. Allan was famished. This affair had his juices going. The vehicle halted.

"Here we are, Marissa."

Once more, she appeared amazed by the crowded yards, vehicles and hostlers, groups of people walking about, and the substantial, white-painted inn. "Oh, it is grand."

Will opened the door; Allan stepped down and reached up for Marissa's hand. She alighted, and he gazed at her fresh, natural beauty. Then he escorted her inside, pleased to have her on his arm.

A harried innkeeper, a white apron covering his bulk, approached them. "Good day, sir and madam."

"Good day. We wish a private room and a meal."

"Certainly, certainly. Step this way, if you will." He toddled along a narrow hall, and they followed.

He led them to a back room filled with sunlight. It seemed clean. A round table and three chairs were there, and it suited Allan. He held Marissa's chair, then he too, sat down.

The innkeeper collected himself, his plump hands on his belly.

"This noon we offer a game pie, a stew of beef shank, and slices of a braised haunch of pork. As well, we can provide a fine vegetable soup. Very hearty, I might relate; I had some for meself." The chap smiled encouragingly.

"I will try the soup, with bread and butter. Give us

your best red wine. Marissa, what will you have?"

"The same, if I may," she murmured.

The innkeeper nodded and left the room, closing the door. Marissa gazed out the window at a tiny pond, in the middle of which sat a brown and green mallard.

"He looks rather old, that duck," she observed. "His feathers are not glossy."

"Nor is his kingdom large," Allan answered.

"He can be an important duck in a small pool," she mused.

"That may suit him better than being an insignificant duck in a big pool."

"Look you," Marissa cried, "he is turning around!"

Slowly, slowly, the duck rocked sideways, then back, then forward, to finally face the other direction.

"Ah, the sun shone in his eyes," he guessed.

"He remembered something he left at home and must go back."

They laughed merrily at this nonsense. Allan felt quite lighthearted, happier than he had been in years. And at last, the food came.

Marissa ate the hot soup with gusto. Amply seasoned, the vegetables were tender and plentiful. She buttered a chunk of bread and ate that, her gaze on Allan. He demolished his soup and a large amount of bread and butter. She wondered if it would be enough for such a big man.

"I suppose you are well over six feet tall, Allan."

"I am. How tall are you?"

"I am unsure. Five feet and a little."

They had another glass of wine from the jug.

"We will stand very close together and see who is tallest," he joked.

She regarded her empty bowl. "I will give you my five shillings. I must pay a share, as I am able. When I cash that draft, Allan, I will give you more."

"Not to trouble. I can pay, Marissa."

"I wish to be fair. You have been more than generous."

"Keep your coins." He drummed his fingers on the table. "I long for a sweet."

"I would like that," she agreed, "and a coffee. Perhaps they have cakes."

As if summoned, the innkeeper tapped and entered. "Finished, are ye?"

"We are. What have you for a dessert?" Allan inquired.

"Our special jam cake, a plum tart, or a baked apple with beaten cream."

"Marissa?"

"The baked apple, please."

"Hmmm. Give the lady that. I will have two slices of the jam cake and bring a pot of coffee."

"Yes, sir. Carrie?" he called.

A serving girl appeared with a tray, removed all the dishes, and left. Marissa loved all of this, the novel food, the busy inn. She might have liked to sit among the other travelers and conjure what their stories were. But still, it was charming to be alone with Allan.

If word of this, er, enforced companionship ever reached Ewell, her reputation would be shredded. It had all been on the up and up, except for those kisses. No one in London would care about her, quite the insignificant duck in that pond.

Carrie labored back in, bearing a tray laden with the sweets, a coffee pot, cups, saucers, sugar, cream, and two forks. She dropped it with a groan and placed the dishes in front of them.

"Mercy," Marissa remarked, "that is a heavy load for you."

"I should say, milady. We had two coaches come in at once, they did. Fair strung us out. There ye be. Enjoy."

Marissa studied her plate, the small baked apple lost under a fat dollop of thick cream. She cut in with her spoon and located the meat of the apple, which seemed a trifle spongey. She poured them each a cup of coffee and added a lump of sugar to hers.

Allan pushed the plate with the second slice of jam cake her way. "Baked apples must be skillfully prepared, or they are shriveled, mushy things. Have this cake."

Surprised, she asked, "Did you order it for me?"

"I did. I am acquainted with poorly baked apples."

"I can bake a fine apple, but they must be eaten promptly." She put the dish aside. "This object may have resided too long in the larder. No matter, I enjoyed the delicious soup, and being here. Thank you, Allan; it is very kind to bring me all this way with you."

"The pleasure is mine. Five miles or so to go." He removed Eban's letter from his pocket and handed it to her. "What think you of this?"

Marissa read. "Why, it is very sorrowful and rings of truth. But written two years ago? Never delivered? To make it up and bring you home again?"

"Stubbins did not say, but I would guess the wench wife sequestered it. Or Eban did, so she would not take it. I hope to find out more when we reach the Hall. Old servants, if they have survived, will have much to share. They will know everything that went on, if the hag did not dismiss them all. But she could not run the Hall alone, the ignorant hussy. It is too large."

It pained her to see his bitterness. "Do not be angry anymore, Allan. Let it go. You said Eban had been unwell. She may have had some terrible influence on an ill man."

"Spineless man. Weak, cowardly," he griped.

"You are young and strong, Allan. Spare a little pity. They are dead and gone."

"Eat your cake," he directed.

Marissa dutifully took a bite, and it tasted good.

****

The coach rumbled along a better road. Allan felt his pulse quicken. The closer they came to the Hall, the more his anticipation increased. At last, the land would be in his hands. Finally, he could take his rightful place among his own, all those who had gone before. He had studied their painted faces since boyhood and knew his kinsmen waited for him.

Allan had tamped down his losses until they had formed a thick block surrounding his heart, like a fish caught in ice. But they could warm enough to swim free, so why could he not do the same? His gaze fixed on Marissa, leaning forward to watch the countryside go by her window. She warmed him, all right. Sometime in the last hours, she had come to stand for, what? The good life.

Allan wished he could again be one and twenty, ready to begin. Full of youthful certainties. But he had been shunted off, shamed, accused, and it had trampled his soul. Time to bloody puff it up again. He would do so by exploring the intricacies of Miss Marissa Barrington's persona. A merry place to begin, he pondered, eyeing her delightful shape. She would fit his arms and his hands and make him come alive again, as once he had been.

He teemed with repressed emotions. He wanted the luscious girl, for one thing, with some urgency. Definitely alive to her, he would get on with it. Take the first opportunity to show her how he felt.

Allan saw the light glint off the fieldstone gates and held his breath. How would it be? In another minute, the carriage turned to the right, passed between them, and entered the boundary of the Hall.

"We have arrived, Marissa."

She said nothing but clasped her reticule and looked to see. The old-growth elms shaded the drive, and Allan glanced about anxiously, fearful ghastly things might have been done to the property. But the drive opened out, and there stood the ancient Hall, straight, solid, and tall, as magnificent as always.

"Ohhh," Marissa breathed.

The afternoon sun burned golden on the banks of windows. The stone façade, a range of grays and creamy tans, was weathered to a patina of age. The three stories rose up into a central tower, and Allan thought it perfection. And all of it appeared to be the same, untouched by the former undeserving tenants.

The carriage circled the drive and stopped at the porch. The roses in full bloom sweetened the air. The porch swept, the grass newly scythed, everything clean, clean, and Allan rejoiced.

Will jumped down and opened the door, his expression cheerful. "Home at last, sir."

"Aye, Will. My thanks to you and Griggs. You will be welcomed by Chance, the stableman, and be made comfortable. Bring the luggage."

He reached for Marissa's hand, and she descended, her face full of wonder.

"Oh, Allan. It is beautiful, all of it. The surrounding land, the extraordinary house."

Pleasure welled up in his chest. "Welcome to Rutledge Hall, Marissa."

A butler dashed from the house, leaving the massive door standing open. "Oh, sir!" he cried. "Welcome, welcome home."

"Norris, old friend," he said, reaching out a hand.

The man took it in both of his, then withdrew. "I must remember my place, but the household has long awaited—forgive me. Please, step in. My boy, bring the cases." He bowed them inside. In the cool of the tiled foyer, Allan introduced Marissa, with great pride.

"Norris, this is my guest, Miss Barrington."

"Ma'am."

"I directed my coachmen to Chance. He is still here?"

"Oh, yes, sir."

Allan could scarcely contain himself. "I am thrilled to find you at your post, Norris. I worried Cordelia would turn everyone out."

The butler became highly annoyed. "No, sir, she could not. The woman riled the town early on by nearly running down a group of children in her phaeton. Then she swore at the frightened babes. Few in Greenhithe would work for her after that, so the old staff remains in place. We all hung fast, waiting for your return."

"Astounding. Well, perhaps Miss Barrington and I could have tea and settle ourselves. If you will bid Mrs. Reid prepare rooms, we will stay until Monday morning. Reid is here? And Merton remains the cook?"

"They are, sir."

"Very good." It all made him lightheaded. "Thank you, Norris."

Allan led Marissa to the drawing room, glancing every which way. Everything appeared to be the same, quite astonishing. The carpets, the paintings, the tables, the rugs. He could scarcely believe it.

"Sit down here, Marissa," he invited, beckoning to the old purple velvet settee by the fire. They both took seats. It seemed as though time had stopped three years ago.

"I am bowled over, I must admit," he explained. "All this time, I have tormented myself with visions of terrible destruction to the house and property. I worried Cordelia would sell off valuables, just for spite. Tear down all that six generations have built. But thus far, it all seems the same."

Marissa smiled, and to Allan, it felt like a blessing.

"Your home is magnificent. I see why it would pain you, Allan, not being here to stand guard. This is your heritage."

She understood! "Yes. It is. I am honor bound to keep it all together and continue the line. That got ingrained as a lad. I had prepared and thought myself ready to take it all on. Then, when the time came to do so, they stole it, right from my hands, with a lie."

Marissa touched his arm. "Remember it is over, Allan. Nothing has been spoiled." She gestured. "This room is pristine."

"And just as I remember it," he marveled. "They seem never to have entered the door."

"You must have a fine housekeeper."

"Mrs. Reid. You will like her, Marissa."

Uncertain, she gazed at him. "Dear me, this is—unusual, my traveling without a maid or a chaperone. What will she think of me?"

Allan placed his hand over hers. "That you are my special friend."

Marissa rapidly became quite unsettled. Everything had ballooned out of shape. Rutledge Hall loomed about three times the size she had expected, embedded like a jewel of architecture in the middle of a vast park. Allan had transformed on his own patch. He seemed even taller and had assumed an intimidating degree of authority. What had happened to the foxy gambler?

Add to that, he now regarded her about the way he had eyed the jam cake before eating it. A rush of icy cold tipped down her back. Had she been addlebrained once again? Had Allan brought her here to, um, ravish her, miles from anywhere? Five shillings would not get her back to London or even to that inn. And if it could, then what? She had a surge of fright and glanced sideways at him.

What sort of ravishment did he have in mind, she recklessly contemplated. No, he would not do anything like that! The faithful servants would know. She would yell for help. He would smother her with—

A tap at the door and in came two maids with tea, their eyes riveted on her, then Allan, then her.

Marissa smiled at them in a friendly manner. "How lovely, Allan."

The two maids smiled back.

"Thank you," Allan said. "I remember you both. Alice, is it not?"

"Yes, sir."

"And Lola."

"Yes, sir. We are all glad you have come home."

"I am glad to be here. Thank you again."

They curtsied and departed.

"Will you pour, Marissa?" he asked.

She did so, filling the flowered china cups. She added one lump of sugar from a silver dish to hers. There were iced ginger biscuits, and she took one, wishing she had never come here. They had enjoyed a friendship of sorts, but it could not endure in this rarified—wait. Something had gone funny. How had Allan inherited this grandeur?

"This is the home you were driven out of?" she asked. "What has changed beside their deaths?"

"Well," he said, munching a biscuit, "I have lost my oppressors and claimed the title. Now, I am the Earl Townshend, like my father and a number of others before him."

Marissa took in this news. Oh, God. The *rules* jumbled in her head. She must leave at the first opportunity.

He raised one brow. "Is that bad?"

"Noooo, I just did not think. I seem to do a lot of that, not thinking. Many congratulations."

"Who is your father?" he pointedly asked. "Tell me."

Very little left to hide, she murmured, "Albert Barrington, Viscount Drake."

He smirked knowingly. "Aha."

She stiffened. "What do you mean, aha? I never presented myself as anyone special or put on any airs."

"You did not have to. Class is stamped all over you. You are a lady of quality, and I saw it immediately."

Marissa sipped her tea.

"Now," he boasted, "by this elevation in my rank, you must curtsey, efface yourself, and call me my lord."

She replaced her cup in the saucer. "And you, sir, may hold your breath until you turn blue."

"Good, good," he praised. "Keep it up. I do like a woman with spunk."

"Spunk," she repeated.

"Grit. Spirit. You have it."

"Developed while boiling turnips, I suppose. Well, now you are enthroned, I must return directly to London if I may and await my aunt."

"You have insufficient funds for that," Allan countered. "Stay, and I will take you to your aunt on Monday. You will be safe here. Shaw is out there, you know, lurking in the shadows, Ludlow right behind him."

How alarming! "He cannot find me here," she stated.

"Exactly, but he will not give up. Therefore."

Marissa tried to reckon with this. What could she do to escape them? Shaw knew where they had been, so he would find out where they had gone and come after her. He would discover Allan had become Lord, um, whatever he said, and come here! She filled with fear.

"I should go, Allan, before one of them comes to make trouble for you. To get even for helping me evade them."

"I can handle that."

"But you should not have to!" she protested. "And in these changed circumstances—"

He munched another biscuit. "I want to. I want you here, with me. In my protection, that is."

Marissa winced, struck with a bolt of suspicion.

Jeanette Collins

Whatever had he said? That he would be her *protector*? Of all the gall. She prepared herself to explode with fury and promptly leave the house.

But another tap sounded at the door, and a silver-haired woman of great presence entered the room. Now she had lost the chance.

Allan jumped up to greet her. "Reid, how good to see you."

They briefly joined hands, and the woman greeted him with pleasure. "Aye, Master Allan. But no more such, now you have come into your own. Below stairs is in a celebration."

He gestured to Marissa. "Allow me to present Miss Marissa Barrington, who has agreed to stay for a couple of nights. To help me adjust."

The woman smiled warmly. "Miss Barrington, welcome. I have prepared a room for you."

"Thank you, Mrs. Reid. I appreciate your trouble."

"If it is convenient, I will show you upstairs."

Marissa glanced his way, then answered, "I would enjoy that."

They left the room. Allan hastened out to speak with Norris, always a font of information, and found him in the back hall sorting candle boxes.

He stood straight. "Yes, my lord?"

"Tell me what has gone on here since I left. Today I received a letter in which Eban apologized, can you believe. He admitted Cordelia had lied about my behavior but wrote it in '15 and never sent it."

He nodded. "Mr. Stubbins collected a number of papers after the funeral. He found no disorder; the estate affairs remained tidy throughout these last years."

"How so? Which of them took charge?"

84

"Her. Once you had been driven out, sir, Mr. Eban's health sank to his boots. She ran everything and ruled his days. Nothing got past her. She kept the books, ordered the steward, Pitts, around, bullied all here, and well, we were saddened to see the Hall in the hands of a harsh woman."

"The place looks just as I left it," Allan murmured in wonder.

"As is the land, so says Pitts."

Allan shook his head. "I do not understand. Why did she not loot the place while she had the chance?"

The butler smiled, justified. "All here observed her every move and saw that she disturbed nothing in the house. We soon learned where her interests lay. She welcomed the profits Pitts produced. She stored up funds, I am sure of it, sir, and paid debts only when pressed. You would never have been granted your inheritance, sir. She meant to take it all, every penny, immediately after Mr. Eban died. Then she would be gone."

"Amazing. She did not sequester the valuables in the safe?"

"Happily, she could not locate the key," Norris confided, removing the iron key from his coat pocket and holding it out.

Allan laughed heartily and took it from his hand.

"We knew you would return, sir. Between all below stairs, Mrs. Reid, Pitts, Chance, and myself, we have kept good track of the estate. And now you are earl." He bowed. "My lord."

Allan, nearly overcome, said, "I am eternally grateful, Norris."

"Yes, my lord."

"One more question. What about this carriage accident that took them?"

Norris assumed a moral stance, his manner disapproving. "She drove that high-perch phaeton mighty reckless, sir. Knew no caution, no matter who else might be on the road. Old Eban said not a word against it. This last fortnight, he took to his bed and naught could get him up again. The doctor summoned gave no hope. But that last day, the fifteenth, a fine Thursday, Mr. Eban wanted to go out for some air. Off they went on the Bridge Road fit to fly; folk thereabout all witnessed the event. She made to overtake a hay wagon, flew off the road, and crashed into the trees."

"I see. Thank you, Norris."

Allan walked away in a state of suspension and climbed the stairs, amazed by the striking developments. He had survived every hardship, then Fate had taken them and spared his legacy. Therefore, Marissa had been proved correct; his exile over, nothing had been spoiled.

Chapter Five

Marissa followed Mrs. Reid, a motherly sort of woman, up a curved set of stairs, the banister carved with a phrase. QUI AUDET ADIPISCITUR, she read, as she ran her fingers over the raised letters. She gazed up at a pair of portraits of two beautiful ladies, lavishly coifed, gowned, and bejeweled. They reached the landing and, partway along a hallway runner of green vines, came to an open door.

"Here we are, miss."

Marissa stepped inside. The white plaster walls were hung with paintings of dogs and horses. A plush Turkey carpet covered the floor in a pattern of reds and blues, the furniture a light wood of some sort, and Marissa loved all of it. The tall windows were flanked by dark-blue drapes in heavy folds. The large bed, covered by a blue paisley comforter, had fat pillows stacked up.

"What a pretty space, Mrs. Reid."

"Aye, and a very fine view; ah, but the light is falling. You will see the garden when you rise. Mina unpacked your valise and will return to help you dress." She folded her hands together, her smile sociable. "Quite a happy day for us. It is so fine to have Lord Allan at home, bringing his lady."

"Well, I am not exactly that," she felt constrained to note. "We are friends, and he asked me to come and see his home." Not a huge lie, Marissa consoled herself.

"I know his ways," Reid stated firmly. "His lordship is a sterling young man, the best. Now he is on the place, we know all will be well again."

"I am very glad."

"Fresh water is there, miss. I will leave you to rest."

"Thank you."

The housekeeper left, closing the door softly. Marissa fell into an overstuffed chair which threatened to swallow her, the room fragrant with lavender. This house seemed practically a castle. Well. Allan had been an earl all along, for years, since his father died. He must have felt mightily betrayed to have it all taken away from him and gone into disguise as a gambler, fooling everyone. He had fooled her, too.

Immediately, her whole chest flooded with sympathy and affection for him. If she had not been sitting, she might have fallen over.

Marissa drew back from this. Not her business. Allan, a kind person, had gone far out of his way for her. He would help anyone in need. And she had fallen short of brilliance, racing headlong for London without so much as a street map. If she had not met him, what would have happened? Maybe something terrible. Like those Egyptians.

Now, he had his home again, and what in the world would he do with her? He must have many tasks, and she would be in his way.

There would be a library. She would take refuge there. Marissa took a deep breath. Allan Rutledge was quite the nicest man she had ever met. A true gentleman. She had nothing to worry about in this palace. Shaw could not find them, and neither could the duke. She closed her eyes and in the quiet, thought of all that had

happened, all that might yet happen, and dozed.
****

Along another hallway, Allan glanced around. He might have been in his room only yesterday. Everything seemed just as he had left it, his books, a stack of letters on the desk he had meant to answer, forgotten when Eban ordered him out. Three years had been removed like a bad tooth. But no, he had lived every day of it in an underworld of shade. Now he would bask in the sunshine.

The puzzle of it lingered. Why had he not been plundered by the bitch, Cordelia? As far as he could see nothing visible had gone missing. *She stored up funds*, Norris had opined, *and only paid debts when pressed*. How interesting. She had wanted cash in hand.

What had Marissa said? *I set money aside…almost like wages…I was keeping the household together*. The greedy Cordelia had surely done the same, on a larger scale. She had skimmed monies from those books she kept, Allan decided. And it could have gone on forever, leaving him in a permanent, cash-strapped limbo.

Where had she hoarded the money? Allan hoped he did not have to knock down a wall to find it, like Marissa's papa. No, Cordelia would not care to dirty her hands. She stashed it here, somewhere in the house, hidden until Eban died and she could escape. The wench had perished before she could steal it away.

He stretched out on his excellent bed and thought of Marissa. The sharp girl would help him retrieve Cordelia's theft. After that, he would take her around the place, get out into the sun, if the weather held. Walk, take a ride, see how the land had fared, and at last, be at home. A dozen things he would like to show Marissa came to his mind. To taste the luxury of ease in her company would be very fine. And he could find if she tired of him in two days. Got restless. Did not care for the country life. Did not care all that much for him.

Jesus. He had become a suspicious man. Marissa more than just liked him; she did, he felt almost sure of it. They had rubbed along well together.

Allan gazed at the ceiling. How long would it take to remember how to be happy? He would ask Marissa. No doubt she would know.

****

Marissa drifted until a soft knock at the door. She came to attention. Mercy. Could it be Allan? "Come."

A brown-haired maid peeped in. "I am Mina."

She stood. "Yes, Mina, please come in. Mrs. Reid said you would help me dress. And you unpacked for me, thank you. I have not brought much."

"Nice things, they are, miss."

"Well. I will wash my face and hands, then wear the amber silk, please, and the leather slippers."

"Yes, miss."

Her traveling gown unfastened and taken away to be brushed, Marissa entered a large dressing room with a pretty marble-topped washstand and washed with a foamy bar of soap that smelled of lemons. The maid handed her a cotton towel. What could she learn of the household?

"Have you worked here long, Mina?" she inquired.

"Two years and four months, when another girl left to be married." She leaned closer. "Mrs. Newton got so mean I often had thoughts to leave myself. Right quick to injure feelings, that lady. Then she drove herself right off the road," Mina indicated, with a sweeping wave of one arm, "and I did not need to seek another position. Otherwise, all here are most kind."

Marissa unlaced and kicked off her half boots. The amber silk, her best, meant to impress her aunt, slid over her. She had not worn it for more than a year, so it seemed almost new. She pushed her feet into the slippers.

"I am good with long hair," Mina offered.

"Oh, wonderful. I am terrible."

The maid laughed softly. "With such lovely hair, it would not matter."

Marissa sat down, and with some skill, Mina brushed and rolled, waved and looped, and fastened it all up again. The glass showed how well the maid had done.

"It is a miracle. I could never do so well. Thank you."

"Yes, miss."

Marissa adjusted the small, puffed sleeves and thought this gown almost as pretty as last night's borrowed raiment.

"I will see you again soon, Mina."

The maid curtsied. Marissa left the room and went down the hall to the stairs full of confidence. Everything kept going wonderfully. She ran her fingers over the inscription as she descended, the house was amazing. All of this impetuous adventure had been amazing. Who would ever have believed any of it could happen?

****

Allan, comfortable in his old dressing room, washed, shaved, and donned a clean shirt. He pulled aside a holland cover, and there hung his old clothes. Disconcerting to see them, as if he had met an old acquaintance thought dead. He had not stopped to take anything that fateful day but had just walked out. Reid, bless her, had kept it all the same.

He opened a bottom drawer. There lay the pistol he had not used, wrapped in a cloth, safely empty. He closed it, feeling two Allans were in the room, one before his exile, and one after. He would merge them and go on.

Allan dressed for dinner out of habit, not even thinking of it. Gazing into the glass, he saw himself back at the Nightingale, with its rank odor of liquor, murky air, and unclean hands. He had the notion to take the garments off again. But that would be tiresome, so he combed his hair and left the room. Soon, he would take over the earl's spacious apartments. On the stairs, he listened for some sound of Marissa but heard nothing.

As he went down, Allan had a moment of abject fear. Now she knew everything. Had it been too much? Had she left? He told himself to be sensible. Unless Marissa had made off with his carriage, coachmen and all, how could she leave?

Not in the drawing room; he walked back to the stairs, and down she came. Allan, washed over with relief, sauntered casually toward her, giving nothing away. Marissa wore a modest gown the color of champagne, her lush red and gold hair all done up in a pretty fashion. Allan had to school his features so as not to betray the fact that she dazzled him. He dug up a guarded compliment, but his emotion spilled over.

"You look lovely," he babbled.

"Thank you. I hoped the gown would be suitable for my aunt."

"What would make it so?" he asked, taking her arm as they strolled to the drawing room.

"The modest neckline."

They took seats on the settee near the fire. Allan thought the garment the most alluring thing he had ever seen.

"You know," she added, "necklines have grown increasingly daring."

"Have they?"

"Yes. Quite so. I have no new things of late but have seen fashion plates. I suppose in London ballrooms, such gowns might be abundant." She looked questioning.

"I have been in no ballrooms for years," Allan grumbled.

"This is too bad. I am sure you dance well."

"If I remember how."

"Of course, you do! If you heard a waltz tune, your feet would move of their own accord."

What things she came up with. It made him restless. "Care for a brandy?"

"Yes, thank you."

Allan stepped to the drinks table and poured two glasses. He would have to check the cellar for intrusions. Maybe Cordelia had tippled and, while sloshed, ran her phaeton off the road. Maybe she had meant Eban to die, and not her. He turned away. Quit thinking of them. They had fallen off the world.

He handed Marissa a glass and sat beside her. She smelled good. He would like to take a big bite of her. What would her flawless skin taste of?

She gazed at him. "I wanted to say, Allan, I know you must have a mountain of things to do. I can amuse myself very well tomorrow, so do not think of me."

Allan wanted to think of her. "I have nothing particular to do. Not yet. Things will rapidly come up, now I am back. The estate is in good shape, Norris told me. It would seem due to the fact Cordelia had her avaricious hands on it all, the estate has prospered."

"Marvelous," she exclaimed. "They did not steal the plate."

"Not exactly. However, I have learned Cordelia has all this time likely been skimming profits and accumulating the money somewhere, her devious plan foiled by a hay wagon. I figure it is in the house and intend to search for it."

Marissa's face became uncertain. Her rosy lips parted.

"It is likely a good deal of cash," he went on. "You are very clever, Marissa. Will you help me search?"

Tears glistened in her hazel eyes.

"It will be like a game," he assured her. She glanced down at her clasped hands. Puzzled, he asked, "Something is wrong?"

Her expression became unutterably sad. "Oh, Allan. If I must deal with another hidden treasure, my heart will break."

Allan realized how it must have troubled her. "Marissa, sweetheart. I promise I will not knock down anything. Come now." What could he do, but put his arms around her? "Really. I imagined we could just snoop around her chamber. I must say, your papa has some kind of boll—nerve to tear down blasted walls."

"I worried blasting would come next." She sighed, her lovely bosom rising and falling softly. "I just—"

"You are so insightful, Marissa," he praised, loving the closeness. "I fancied you could set your mind to the problem and go right to the spot." Allan assumed a fatigued pose. "I am just a dull fellow when it comes to a mystery."

She laughed softly. "Oh, what a fib. What is carved on the stair rail?"

"Latin. The Rutledge motto. *Qui audet adipiscitur*."

"What does it mean?"

"*Qui* means who. *Audet*, from the Latin *audex*, means daring, or bold. The Latin *adipiscor* means to acquire or obtain. Therefore, it all comes around to 'Who Dares Wins.' "

"Oh, gosh."

"I applied it to my gambling career. Which is over and done with."

"I am glad." She sipped the drink. "Language is very important to you, I think."

Another one of her perceptive jolts prodded him.

"Not just English," she said. "Your manner changed when you talked about Latin. You were speaking of a deep love for words."

Allan struggled to maintain his poise and gulped down his brandy.

"You must have received a fine education at Oxford, Allan. I do envy you that."

"More brandy?" he croaked, as if strangling.

She held up her glass, her face angelic. "Please. It is like drinking sunshine."

Allan would promptly implode if she did not be quiet. He poured the brandy with an unsteady hand. Marissa Barrington had attempted to see into his soul. He felt vulnerable; she carried a blade of searing intimacy. He could hardly return fast enough, to endure more of her verbal surgery.

Marissa knew she had likely said too much, accepted the brandy, and vowed to be still.

In a moment, Allan began to talk. "The fact is,

Marissa," he related in a serious tone, "as a student, I became deeply involved in the growing field of linguistics. The study of languages, their origins, and usage in thought processes and communication between peoples."

She filled with admiration. "How lovely."

"For a time, I meant to devote myself to this scholarship, but the estate remained on my mind. How were matters going? The crops, the tenants, all of it. I heard nothing from Eban. I worked on, took that extra term I mentioned, and reached my majority. I decided I could do both, run the Hall properties and research to my heart's content. I came home to find that had been a hollow dream."

Marissa, eager to know his dreams, listened with every pore.

Allan's face became very young and gloomy. "I watched it all go flat in London. The books I read and the papers I planned slipped away in the night. My mind went completely empty." He glanced away, evidently still in the grip of his losses.

She had to speak. "It all waits for you to come back, Allan. Things you value stay in your mind, like your memory for cards. A skill for remembering is a gift, and you have it. I know language can be a dear companion, like my letter to a friend. I may call it a poem, but it is always beloved words linked together. Language is an endless pleasure."

Allan looked rather dumbfounded.

"If that makes any sense," she amended.

A silence fell. Marissa made her drink last. Allan kept his gaze on her. A log fell in the fire, and sparks rose like fairies, on wings of flame. She scraped up conversation.

"What was your father like, Allan?"

He grinned. "A windstorm. He went at life with tremendous energy and tended to be noisy and opinionated. He was always a tremendously kind, understanding, generous man with monies and time. Everyone, including me, loved him dearly. Father enjoyed sport and rode to hounds, hunted, and liked a party. He adored my mother, a gentle, rather wistful, youngest daughter of a Shropshire marquess. Father met her when she was presented at court at the age of seventeen.

"It took three years for my father to marry her, but he did. He always said it took that long because he did not wish to rob a cradle. She died when, like you, I reached fifteen. One morning—" Allan grimaced. "—she did not wake up, the most terrible event that had ever happened to us. Father was never the same man after that; in less than two years, he too, died."

"How dreadful, Allan. In the midst of such happiness."

Of all things, he leaned to her and rested his head on her shoulder. "Comfort me," he murmured.

Marissa reached up and smoothed his rich and silky dark hair. She felt his warm breath and caressed his cheek, his skin firm, textured, and wonderful to touch. A bit cramped, and not in a position to do more, she judged his weight. It all made her giddy.

In a deft move, he changed places and now held her. "How do I comfort you, pretty Marissa?" He smoothed *her* hair and caressed *her* cheek, his expression impish.

"Well, I had been hoping for dinner."

Instead, Allan kissed her lips, his mouth incredibly

soft and gentle.

Allan fell into Marissa like a penny into a pocket. Her mouth sweet and giving, she showed no coyness or guile and kissed him with an open heart. He flew free of constraint for an uncharted distance, reached for more, and a tap at the door ended the reverie.

Marissa eased away as Norris entered. "My lord, dinner is served."

"Very good, Norris."

Allan helped Marissa stand. She weighed nothing; he could scale the stairs in a trice with the delicious creature in his arms. However, her face became a question he could not answer. He had no idea what he should do, he just wanted all of her. He led her to the dining room; his sentiments stirred up fit to overset him.

The large, airy room had never looked better to Allan. Filled with past good times, it still contained the presence of loving family, boundless security, and all the rest he had known as a boy. Of his boisterous father and the fragile grace of his mother. He held Marissa's chair, bending to inhale her scent. Lemons, warm flesh, and desirous woman filled his lungs.

Allan went on high alert. Must keep his wits. This country girl had changed to an enchantress. He took the chair at the head of the long, polished table very much the earl. She would not get the best of him, now the one in charge of everything for miles around.

George, the old footman, served a clear soup. "George," Allan said with pleasure, "I am happy to see you again."

A cheery smile. "As we all are to see you, sir."

"It is grand to be home." And he meant it.

George poured the wine, and Allan had a good

drink. His favorite white Burgundy.

Marissa tasted her soup. "Mmmm, very rich flavors."

"The cook, Mrs. Merton, is splendid."

She sipped the wine. "This is the wine Murray served."

Allan became instantly defensive. "I like it. It has some weight."

She only smiled. Her lovely face made the candles fade. He had to get a firmer hold on himself. Forget sitting at a card table, his livelihood on the line. It had just been an exceedingly long time since he had, what? Cared about a woman? Felt such scorching desire? Yearned to hold Marissa for about the next ten years?

Allan had valued his ability to reject the lower kinds of women he had lately encountered. A proud man, not to say arrogant, it would have soiled his mind to give in to tawdry lust. So, he had done without. Parts of him had been sacrificed in the process, along with any kind of intimacy, which involved trust. Who could be trusted?

Now he had become smitten, whacked in the heart by this feminine, tempting, disorienting invasion by the other side. He had helped her into that scruffy mail coach and lost his moorings. Since then, his boots had not touched solid ground.

Allan absently ate his fish. Marissa delicately tasted everything twice, it seemed to him. The food, the wine. She savored things. It gave him a quiver along his spine. The maids removed dishes, and the footman brought in the main course. George prepared a roast of pork for their plates, and maids offered various other dishes and poured a red wine, a Pinot Noir variety.

The table held everything he had enjoyed in the past,

and Allan served himself large portions. He had an enormous appetite, he realized, and glanced to see Marissa carefully sampling her food. Allan proceeded to stuff himself. She brought him good medicine and made him want some of absolutely everything. It had been bloody good luck to encounter her, no doubt about it.

Marissa thought it a wonderful meal. Not being required to cook any of it enhanced her enjoyment. Fresh herbs had been used, the pork was juicy, extra tender, and the red wine superb, with a full body. Likely a Pinot from the Bordeaux region. She ate heartily and liked it all.

"There must be a fine cellar here," she ventured.

"Indeed, there is, and I am confident the butler kept it secure. The Newtons were hemmed in by the staff, according to Norris. Keys were sequestered. Therefore, we are more or less intact in all respects."

"How fine of them. Our small staff bolted for the road when wages became scarce. I could not fault them. After Miss Grisham went, I rather lost heart. I watched it all go by in a state of disbelief mingled with resignation. Painful to be so powerless."

His dark eyes bright, he leaned eagerly toward her. "I found myself in the same state, Marissa. I never expected to live on too low an income to keep a parrot. Never mind my name, my rank became useless if I lacked money. I had to seriously readjust. I acquired the services of Murray, who likes to eat every day and wear clothes, and needed even more cash."

Allan suddenly laughed. "It caused me some consternation, but I soon resorted to my only ability and stepped down into an inferno to gamble."

This, Marissa found difficult to imagine. Awful

scenes went through her mind. "Oh, Allan. How horrible for you."

He shrugged. "Once or twice, it threatened to be fatal. Many times, I despaired, lost in my predicament. But hi, ho. Aside from the bad air, exclusive clubs were padded with luxury. If you were admitted, that is. I had all the trappings of an aristocrat, strolled right in, and proceeded to win the money of other like gentlemen—which, in the main, I knew they would never miss."

"In the main?" she questioned.

"Mostly. Some men rashly think they are highly skillful and foolishly sit down with better players."

"It sounds risky," Marissa breathed.

"Indeed. People become very touchy when you win their money. I did not cheat; I had no card up my sleeve. Nothing concealed, ever. My ability to count the deck made me the superior player in a ruthless game. And I needed the money."

They went on eating.

Allan's face brightened. "I admit it could become tricky. Once, an Italian *conte* joined the loo table, whom I quickly realized to be a professional. I got into a fix. The wagers got larger and larger, pushing me up against it. If I lost, I would be exposed, would have to bow out, and this would ruin my reputation as a wealthy man. I watched every move, every gesture, waiting for my chance. The wagers came very rapidly.

"Then he made a mistake. He quickly glanced around the table and faintly whispered, *diciotto*, *venti*; eighteen, twenty. I heard, knew he had been counting cards but had lost the count and become blind. Play went around the table, and once again, he faltered. I laid down my cards at the right moment and won everything."

"*Qui audet adipiscitur*," she recited.

"It is the only way."

Allan seemed to grow loftier in Marissa's estimation, all while sitting there. How bold and daring. High stakes gambling had been an insane situation for him to get into, but nonetheless, he'd ventured.

She was certain he could handle anything that came along and admired his boldness. What a courageous man, to face his opponents and triumph. It made her weak.

Once again maids quietly gathered dishes and poured a tawny Sauterne as George brought in dessert. A beautifully browned meringue floated on a richly yellow egg custard.

"How pretty, George," Marissa exclaimed.

"Thank you, miss."

"Indeed, it is, George," Allan agreed.

Marissa, delighted, dipped her spoon, and tasted citrus and a hint of rum. The sweetened meringue dissolved in her mouth. "Perfection," she murmured.

She wasted no time consuming this treat. Drank the excellent Sauterne, a feast in itself, and felt full to the top. "Such a wonderful meal, Allan. All of it, every bite. Should I go downstairs and help with the dishes?"

"No more of that, my dear." He reached for her hand. "Your hand is soft and smooth with no pots to scrub." He turned it over, raised it to his lips, and kissed her palm. Marissa shivered, unprepared for the trail of hot electricity that traveled up her arm. Unsettled, she slowly dragged it away from him.

He grinned. "Very kissable, in fact."

George presented himself.

"George," Allan said, "a splendid meal. The wine choices suited it all. Do compliment Merton."

"I will, sir. Shall I serve coffee in the drawing room?"

"Please." Allan rose and reached again for her hand. Marissa stood and left the room on his arm, unsure what he had meant by such an intimate liberty. It may have exposed her in some unknown way. And she knew Allan knew he had done so. She had better watch him even more closely. If that could be possible.

Allan realized kissing Marissa's palm had been too much. It had plowed up all sorts of painful longings. Damn it, he had been getting along in his rigid celibacy, had he not? Then she had appeared, had spoken, and promptly knocked his monkish discipline askew. Now he could only think of spiriting her up to his chamber and—

In came one of the maids with the coffee tray, placed it on the low table, and silently departed. Without a word, Marissa poured and handed a cup to him. This quiet act engulfed Allan in a scene of domestic bliss that made him feeble. He had never thought such a situation would appeal to him so strongly.

His parents had loved each other, Allan had seen it. But that had been them; they were special, in his boy's eyes. That did not signify he would find such a partner to share his life with. As heir to an earldom, he had been approached by every female able to stand up without assistance, but Allan had been lighthearted. He had enjoyed the company of young women that appealed to him and intended to go right on doing so as earl. Then the sky had fallen on his head.

Allan had encountered no such fine ladies in gambling hells and had turned away from the rabble. Murray had been the only close contact he had allowed himself. Except for Stubbins, his ally since school days. Now everything had changed. At last free, he could pick up his life where he had left off. Perhaps Marissa would be interested in…He glanced at her.

She gazed into the fire, warming her hands with her cup. The curve of her cheek captivated his attention. The downy softness, the youthful color. The cleanliness. He must walk softly. To violate such adorable innocence would be a cardinal sin. To possess it would be a rare prize.

Loud voices from the foyer. Allan listened. Marissa gazed at him. "Wait," he said, and walked rapidly to the doors. Opened one and stepped out, closing it again.

"What is it, Norris?"

"Men at the door, my lord. Demanding to see you."

Allan guessed who it might be. "Let them in but reveal nothing."

Norris cautiously opened the door. There stood an obviously livid, crimson-faced Mr. Shaw; two mean-looking fellows, each of them possibly larger than Murray, were with him.

Allan immediately bellowed, "What is the meaning of this?"

Shaw drew himself up virtuously, though still short. "You have failed to evade me, sir! I am not to be swayed from my lawful duty to His Grace. I readily found who you are, where you went, and have come to retrieve Miss Barrington. I shall not relent or give up and intend to take her from here. With force, if necessary."

Allan stood tall. "The devil you say. Although I have no obligation to do so, I must inform you that Miss Barrington, by this hour, is safely in Bath, to be supervised by her aunt. If you were indeed diligent, you would know said aunt is there for the cure. Therefore! Never darken my door again, raise hell, and upset my household on a trifle, or I will set the dogs on you."

Shaw, visibly taken aback, rubbed his chin with chubby fingers. "Bath?" he murmured.

"Get yourself and these two bruisers off my property," Allan ordered. "Norris, close the door."

Norris slammed it in their faces.

"I will explain later," Allan murmured.

"Yes, my lord."

He hurried back to Marissa. This required a fast plan. He had no intention of letting her be delivered like a side of beef to that wearisome bastard duke. Never.

****

Marissa heard the entire exchange and had gotten to the floor. She crouched there, hoping not to be seen if someone looked in the windows. Allan yelled in a heroic manner as he told Shaw a bouncer. Her heart flooded with warmth; also, she had gotten too close to the fire. She crawled farther away just as Allan rushed back in.

"Marissa?"

"Down here."

He knelt beside her, and she sat up.

"I feared to be seen. Who could credit this? Are all men fanatics?"

"Most of us." Allan stood again, went around the room, and extinguished all the lamps.

Marissa straightened her gown. He came back and sat beside her on the floor. They leaned back on the settee and stretched their feet toward the fire.

"Well," Allan said, "with luck, they are on the way to Bath."

"They?"

"Shaw had two large fellows with him, in case Murray should appear."

She held her head in both hands. "Oh, how horrible this has all become," she mourned. "I will have to emigrate to the savage Americas."

"Not to worry. We have three directions to go. One, the London house. Shaw is not likely to return there and encounter Murray. Two, stay here and lie low. This does not suit me. I will not hide out on my own land. Or three, we, too, can journey to Bath and catch up your storied aunt."

Marissa protested, "Nooooo. We do not know where in Bath she is stopping. By the time we get there and attempt to find her, she may be on her way back to London. I choose Murray and the house. One more night there, then I will go to my aunt and her raucous cat."

A silence stretched out. Marissa now felt a bit desperate. "Oh, Allan. The duke will give up, will he not? Who would want someone who has to be hunted down? I will drown myself before I let him touch me."

"Hush. It will not come to that. I will kill him."

"Absurd notion!" she cried.

"It is a thought. I would be your knight in shining armor."

"Ha. You wear a suit of armor already."

One expressive brow lifted. "Eh?"

"To prevent anyone from giving you cuddles."

He laughed in a surprised way. "Cuddles, is it? *Cuddles*?"

"Hugs. Embraces. I imagine they have naught of that in gambling establishments."

"I should say not. I would worry they had the pox." He gazed intently at her. "I formed the habit of doing without affection. I had no one like you to help me remember."

Marissa reached out and took his hand. So much larger than hers. Rough surfaced. She twined her fingers with his. When this became inadequate, she lifted it to her lips and kissed the back of his hand. Dark hair grew along the side of it and tickled her nose. Allan put his arm around her, and they sat there in the quiet, as the fire leapt and snapped.

Allan relaxed, massively content, but he longed to sleep with Marissa. He knew with her beside him, he could at last rest. Sleep the night through and wake refreshed. It had been an age since he had done so. Just to share her warmth, her fragrance, her very presence would soothe him. Not necessarily make love with her. Unless she wanted to. Which she would. He would see to that.

He quickly went the other way. What? He met the girl yesterday! Then the world had slanted over. Stubbins's revelations, his tormentors erased, his so-called crime expunged. Allan did not know when it all coalesced, but Marissa had become an important part of the upheaval. He felt bound to her by ties of circumstance and a rattling chain of desire.

He saw nothing else to do. He would prevent the duke from having so much as a glimpse of Marissa. Allan intended to keep her for himself. He would arrange this carefully, and before she had time to think, she would be his. Take the gamble he could get her to love him, warts and all, so to speak.

Of course, Marissa would consent to all of this. It would solve her problem and his. If she agreed. But would she? She would not care to exchange one restraint on her freedom for another.

Yet, when he kissed her, she expressed no resistance whatsoever, and this encouraged him.

"Allan," she whispered.

"Yes, my dear?"

"I cannot stay awake any longer."

"Then I will see you to your room."

They untangled themselves and stood up. Allan took her arm, warm, soft, and they proceeded to the foyer in the shadows. Only one lamp burned on the hall table. Allan lit a candle; they headed to the stairs and silently climbed.

At the landing, she spoke. "Thank you, Allan, for everything. If not for you, I would be back in Ewell. Locked up somewhere until the vicar could be summoned."

"It will not happen, Marissa, if I can help it."

They turned down the hall to her door. "How can I ever repay your kindness?" she asked, her expression troubled.

He had to smile. "I will think of something. How about a kiss good night, then we will be even?"

"Please."

Allan folded her in his arm, balanced the candlestick, took one whole second to look into her hazel eyes and inhale the scent of her hair, then he kissed her lips. The house rocked. His pulse increased; his heart thumped. He became uncertain of his balance and teetered there, holding her. Kissing her. For a moment, owning her thoughts.

Marissa melted into him, and he felt her every shapely curve. This is *it*, he shouted inwardly. She had become the only woman for him, now and always. To his astonishment, she slipped away.

"Oh, my gracious, Allan," she breathed.

"I could not help myself. You are enchanting, Marissa."

"Thank you, but—"

"I went slightly overboard. I did not mean—"

"Well, I certainly did. Good night, Allan." She opened the door and lamplight spilled out.

"Sleep well."

The door softly closed. Allan turned to leave, and the candle snuffed. In the dark, he groped along the hallway toward his room. Without Marissa, he mused, he had no light. He would fix that. He needed her in his life. Tomorrow, he would begin to play the odds and, with all his skills, would win her.

****

Marissa drifted sleepily across her chamber. Whatever had Allan been up to? It may be, she thought as she undressed, that he felt lonesome. No, that could not be all of it. Or the excitement of finally coming home had overwhelmed his good sense. Or he just enjoyed kissing. Maybe he secretly liked her? The idiot duke and his mindless pursuit suggested she had some appeal. She washed her face and hands and this time, feeling secure, donned her nightie. Marissa extinguished the lamps and climbed into the very large bed. She pulled the soft comforter over her and relaxed. Moonlight filtered into the room. The linens smelled faintly of lavender.

Allan had become very romantic. He liked those cuddles after all, although he had scoffed at the term. So fun to talk to, to be with. Some woman would be very lucky to find him. Be his and all of that. Live in this fine house she had seen a corner of. Where he would never knock down the walls.

This escapade would soon end, best prepare for that. Then what she would do eluded her. She had depended on her aunt to guide her, which seemed like mindless nonsense now. She had better keep her own counsel. The problem with that, her vast ignorance. Just keep going, see what happens. For the present, she thought happily, she would sleep in Allan's unbelievably fine house, his true home. Tomorrow would take care of itself.

Marissa thought of his kiss, of his particular, manly scent, dozed, and borne away by a dream of Allan's love, slept.

Chapter Six

Sunday

Allan woke with a start as someone entered the room. He sat up, ready for trouble. God above, his old valet!

"Gates!" he exclaimed. "Can it be?"

A wide smile creased the features of the tallish, slender man. "It is I, my lord. I have brought your coffee."

He accepted the cup. "Where have you been all this time?" Allan asked.

Gates's open countenance became downcast. "Pressed into service to Mr. Newton, sir, but he proved unwilling, then unable, to allow me to do so. I retreated below stairs and took up other duties. We all found it advisable to avoid any interaction whatsoever with Mrs. Newton."

"Quite so. I am more than glad to have you back, Gates."

"Yes, sir. It has all come around right at last." A look of disdain crossed his features. "They were not, if I may say, the best sort of people."

"I agree. The wife siphoned off estate profits, I suspect, while waiting for Eban to die."

"I would not doubt it, sir. She appeared a grasping sort."

111

"Well, welcome back, Gates. I have this other little problem to sort out. My schedule is uncertain, but I intend to be in residence from now on." Allan had to seclude Marissa. "However, I must journey back to London today. A friend is staying in the house, and she must return to town."

"Very well. A bath, sir?"

"By all means. I have a lot to do today."

Gates saw to this as Allan drank his coffee. He glanced around the large room, then realized he had slept the whole night without interruption! For years, he had sorely missed a good night's rest. He had thought being in Marissa's arms might let him sleep soundly, but just having her in the house, nearby, seemed enough. Marvelous! He leapt out of bed, energy bubbling up in his chest.

The morning rituals complete, Allan descended the stairs, clean as a babe.

Norris, on duty in the foyer, beamed. "Good morning, my lord."

"Norris. How goes it?"

The butler leaned toward him, his expression concerned. "One of them is still out there, sir."

"One of whom?"

"Those ruffians from last night. I saw him, my lord. The fellow has a horse tied up and is just standing there, beyond the row of forsythia bushes. I believe he stayed the night, watching."

"Think of that. I must confide in you, Norris. It is quite a story. Miss Barrington is being pursued to the point of madness by a duke so fixated on her, he will go to any lengths to carry her away. The short blockhead last night, Shaw, is his lackey."

Norris gaped. "A *duke*?"

"Well, she hates him, and he is not going to have her. I am taking the lady back to London, playing for time. Her aunt will return from Bath tomorrow, and Miss Barrington will be in safe hands. Maybe. I do not know; I am blundering along."

"I am certain you will be effective, sir," Norris encouraged.

Allan determined he would be. He had luck, innate skills, and a parade of ancestors, a few of whom were known, when necessary, to be cutthroats. Allan, the seventh Earl Townshend, would not be mucked about with. Ludlow would never have the chance to touch Marissa Barrington. His life on it.

****

Marissa woke to rustling sounds of movement and opened her eyes, heavy with sleep. She sat up.

"Good morning, miss."

"Ah, Mina," she groggily said. "Good morning."

"I brought a cup of chocolate."

"Did you?" Marissa exclaimed, taking the cup. "Wonderful." She sipped the foamy, almost bitter brew and woke up. "Perfect."

"It is a fine day. Shall you have a bath?"

"Oh, yes, that would be lovely. Um, what is the time?"

"Just gone seven."

"Amazing. I never sleep so late. Have I missed breakfast?"

"I think not, miss. I will see to the bath."

Marissa had slept like the dead, the blanket of night tucked around her. This house seemed a fortress, and Allan rested nearby, her knight in armor, shiny or no. She

113

loved this fanciful notion and drained the cup.

Soon, she soaked in an oval brass tub, while Mina did all the work. Practically disgraceful to be so idle, but Marissa sat there anyway, imagining an uncertain future. She had forgotten the sheer indulgence of being waited upon. It had been buried beneath potato peelings.

"Is your home nearby, Mina?" Marissa asked, beginning to wash with a fragrant ball of lemony soap.

"Yes, miss. Our farm is some two miles distant."

"Ah, so you did not need to leave your home."

"I would have done, if the chance had come. But the wage here is good, and the family profits." The girl smiled in a lively way, her blue eyes merry. "As well, I do not have to tend the cows and poultry. I get an elevated quality of life, as Mr. Norris says. This pleasure grew some thin for the household under the Newtons, being the missus could be mean as a badger. All agree his lordship will set everything to rights, now he has come home."

"I am sure he will."

Marissa stepped out of the water and dried off. Mina presented clean underthings. She sat at the dressing table while the maid brushed, combed, swirled, and wrapped, transforming Marissa's hair.

"Impressive, Mina. You have great skill."

"Thank you, miss."

Marissa dressed again in the blue carriage gown, anticipating a trip back to the city. She laced her half boots, checked the glass once more, thanked the maid, and left the room. She descended the stairs and saw Allan standing below, speaking with Norris. He turned, their gaze met, and her heart swelled in her chest. With a smile, he came to the stairs to meet her.

"Here you are, Marissa. Good morning."

"Good morning, Allan. Mr. Norris."

The butler nodded.

Allan took her arm; they strolled down the hall and turned into a sunny breakfast room, gauzy curtains at the windows. The pale-yellow walls reflected the light and dappled the table.

Rich food smells made her stomach pinch. They stepped to a sideboard and covered, silver dishes. Allan lifted one.

"Eggs. Have some, Marissa."

She took a spoonful of whipped eggs. They moved along offerings of bacon, sausages, and kippers. All for two people, Marissa mused, eyeing dishes of sliced berries, fresh scones, and clotted cream. She filled her plate, as did Allan, and they took seats. A maid poured coffee, and they began to eat.

"So much food," she murmured, while enjoying it.

"No one goes hungry here. I assure you, any excess will be enjoyed below stairs. The help eat well, Merton sees to that, and many workers come in for a bite during the day. Or they used to. Meantime, we are blessed with plenty for all."

"It is truly a blessing," she agreed.

"I am more mindful of this than before." Allan leaned her way, his face youthful, his dark eyes luminous. "Did you sleep well last night, Marissa?" he asked.

"Why, yes, I did. I slept later than usual and woke only when the maid entered the room. She brought me a delicious cup of chocolate."

"I must tell you that I slept wonderfully. Deep, dreamless, and restful. Sleeplessness has plagued me in my exile."

She smiled, pleased for him. "Now you will be happy again, Allan."

"I will," he earnestly said, "if you are nearby."

Marissa felt her cheeks grow hot, bit into a scone, and clotted cream dribbled. Allan reached out and wiped a bit from her chin, then he licked the cream from his finger! It took her breath away.

Allan gave her no chance to object to this audacious gesture and announced, "We will return to London later today. I would like to spend an hour searching Cordelia's chamber. After that, there is a spot of problem we must deal with."

Lawsy, now the earl readily gave orders. "What is that?" she warily asked.

"I told you Shaw had two brutes with him last night. One stayed behind to watch the house and is still out there."

Her hand went to her breast in alarm. "Oh, no!"

"Well, my dear, it is about the dumbest plot I ever heard of. Obviously, he is hanging about to see if you leave the Hall. And then what? He would follow us to London on horseback? The carriage will leave him in the dust."

Marissa became thoughtful. "No, that cannot be right. I have it; Shaw and the other man went back to the Crescent Inn for the night. If I attempt to leave, this one will ride to the inn, notify Shaw, and they will take out after me."

Allan judged the risks involved. "But what if you are not seen to leave? What if we spirit you out of the house?"

"In a trunk?" she gasped.

Allan laughed at this notion.

"Or I could dress like someone else," she suggested. "A man. Or one of the maids."

He dismissed this. "The thug would spot you in a minute by your hair."

"Well, then, what can we do to get away? Roll me up in a carpet like Cleopatra?"

"And bruise your fair person? Nay. I reckon we must overwhelm him. I will call for every vehicle on the place, and we will all drive away at once. At some point, the others will turn back and block the road. Our visitor will be stymied, and on we will go."

"That would be terribly elaborate," Marissa mused, "like raising an army. How about this—Mina told me this morning that her home is about two miles from here. If she would, she could dress like me, cover her hair, and be driven off, leading this man away from us. When Mina arrives at her home, he sees his mistake, but it is too late. Meanwhile, we have sprinted for London."

Allan liked Marissa's clever plan. The girl had a brain. Maybe better than his. "That sounds plausible," he agreed.

She drained her cup. "What a comedy. Shaw must be all at sea. It is rather humorous to observe him running in circles. As well, my missing aunt knows not a whit of all this, that I ran away and am touring England. My father is back in Ewell, digging, no doubt, and may not have missed me. The duke has sent his minion after us, while I am suspended above the ground, neither here nor there."

He fondly regarded her. "I know where you are, Marissa."

"In your house?"

"In the cosmos. In my affectionate regard."

He observed Marissa weigh this remark, then dismiss it. "How nice you are to say so, Allan. It quite boosts my confidence that I actually exist in the world, and someone can see me. I will find my place, I promise, and you will be proud to hear of it."

Allan vowed to increase his amorous efforts when able. "I am proud of you now." They stood from the table. "Let us put our plan in motion. First, a search, then you will find Mina and see if she agrees to help us."

"I shall."

She smiled, warming his heart. Of course, Marissa did not know how much he had come to care for her. Best keep that to himself for the present, but it had become difficult to do so. Loving words demanded to be said. Keep your temperature down, Allan lectured himself, or you will boil over.

Allan led the way down the hall past the dining room until they came to closed double doors. He opened them wide, then stood there in the doorway, his dour expression annoyed and offended. Marissa waited.

"Eban being unwell," he finally said, "the stairs were difficult, so they settled on this floor and spared the earl's apartments from contamination."

They strolled inside a small sitting room. Marissa thought it very luxurious, with a sky-blue crushed-velvet settee and pretty upholstered chairs arranged before a fireplace, now standing cold. There were no pictures on the walls, and nothing adorned the mantel. More than just vacant, it seemed to her no one had ever lived here.

"Eban's chamber," Allan said, pointing to the left, "and Cordelia's is this way."

They moved to the second door, and Allan opened

it. A bedchamber, with that same stale air of emptiness. Again it seemed a fine room, the bed covered in a patterned quilt, a pretty upholstered chair beside it. The dressing table stood bare of articles, save for an ivory comb. Nothing personal, no trinket or favorite object on display anywhere.

"How barren she made things," Marissa murmured.

"Cordelia sucked the juice out of everything she touched," Allan remarked, his voice flat, "and stored it all up in her gut, like some hideous animal."

"Oh, dear."

He turned to her. "Well, it is true!" Then he sighed deeply. "Never mind all that. I need to forget both of them."

"Ill of the dead, and all," Marissa agreed.

With that, he laughed heartily. Marissa approved of this. If Allan could laugh, he had recovered his good humor.

"How can we find anything in an empty room?" she murmured.

He strolled to the dressing room, and she followed. Cordelia's meager wardrobe hung there. Black and brown gowns, a black pelisse, and a brown marled woolen robe. On a hook, a beige flannel nightgown with a tear at the hem. Below that, a rack of plain slippers and a pair of worn, brown half boots.

"She did not like colors, it seems," Marissa guessed. She reached out to touch them. "And these garments are far from new. It is all very frugal, Allan. If she took monies, it did not go for gowns and fripperies."

Allan began to pull open the row of shallow drawers. Most contained a dreary array of chemises, stockings, and the like, all in the same degree of advanced wear. Marissa did not like poking through someone else's things, even if they were dead. Actually, that made it worse.

"There is nothing here," she ventured.

"No," Allan agreed. "Not that we can see."

They returned to the bedchamber. To Marissa's amusement, Allan knelt down and carefully searched under the bed. She stepped to the dressing table and gazed in the mirror, which tilted to one side. She pinched her cheeks, smoothed her hair, then absently reached out to straighten it, but the frame had caught on something.

She stepped to the side, studied it, and pushed one edge. To her horror, a wrenching creak sounded; Marissa quickly stepped aside as the entire glass pitched forward, fell with a crash onto the table, then flipped over to land on the rug in a hail of glass fragments.

Allan rushed to her side and grabbed her arm. "Marissa! Are you all right, darling?"

Shaken, she answered, "Yes, yes, I am so sorry." She gestured. "I just meant to—"

They looked to the wall. A large picture hook dangled free. Below it, inserted in the plaster, a brass door about a foot square, with a keyhole.

"A safe," Allan said triumphantly. "The witch installed a safe to hide her plunder!" He fell on her for a hug. "And you found it," he said. "You walked right to it."

"Well, I—um, the frame had gone crooked."

"So had Cordelia. Hmmm. Now we need the key." Allan sedulously studied the room.

Marissa thought what she would do, then said, "If all my ill-gotten gains were in that safe, I would never part with the key. When the Newtons, um, went, what happened to their things?"

"Eh?"

"Their clothes and shoes, a timepiece, wedding rings, or a bit of jewelry? What happened to them?"

"Norris will know," Allan exclaimed. "Let us go down and speak to him."

He took her hand, and they hurried to the stairs. *Darling*; Allan had called her darling. Only because he thought she might be hurt. Yes. That explained it.

****

"The clothing being in a sorry state, Woolrich, the undertaker, discarded the lot, my lord. The personal things that remained I put on the library desk until I knew your wishes."

"Too grand, Norris. Just the thing." Allan tugged Marissa that direction. He had not stepped a foot in the library for years. He opened the door and hastened in. Forcefully struck by a wave of sentiment, his stomach turned over. He saw his father sitting at the big cherry desk, as clear as if he were alive. The vision disappeared. The years, the wasted years; his father would never come again.

He let go of poor Marissa's hand, which he had been clutching, and leaned on the wall. A long moment passed.

She touched his sleeve. "Are you well, Allan?"

"Yes. Yes, it is just, it is all over. The Newtons, the years of anxiety trying to keep myself intact; my good father gone, my mother long since. My youth dried up like water."

"Everyone's youth fades before we know. Yesterday, I was twelve and in my mother's arms. I had no more awareness at the time than a simpleton, of what

I had and what I would lose. Anyway, Allan, you are very young. Everything is ahead of you."

"Why do I feel old?" he whispered.

"Because, perhaps, under terrible pressures, you forgot how to be carefree."

Allan, immediately relieved, knew it could all happen; no painful loss would stop him or make him too late for anything. "Marissa," he said, turning to embrace her. "You are a revelation."

"Oh, well."

"Come, let us see what Norris left."

They stepped to the big desk. An envelope lay there, addressed to him. He tore the end and dumped out the contents. Marissa craned to see. He picked up a narrow gold ring; inside were engraved initials, E to C. They both studied it. Then a chain of heavy silver links with a cat's eye fob, attached to a silver pocket watch. The case badly bent, it had stopped at twenty minutes past two. And lastly, on a thin leather cord, hung a brass key.

"Such a few things to leave behind," Marissa remarked.

Allan gazed down at the spare items, then at Marissa, who made everything hopeful again. "Shall we go and see what she hid?"

"I guess so."

"Doubts?" he asked.

"About hidden things. It may not be a treasure."

"I want nothing but my own back, Marissa," Allan protested. "If she nicked the profits, I have a right to recovery."

"True. Then let us go and find out what warranted a safe. It rather damaged the wall."

"Walls again." He laughed.

They climbed the stairs and once more entered the room. Scattered glass twinkled in the light from the windows. Stepping around it, Allan inserted the key and turned it. The lock tumblers clicked smoothly, and the door swung open. Marissa stood closer, eager to see what it contained. Allan peered in and removed a thick sheaf of documents. He looked at the heavy lines of engraving and an ornate seal.

"Bank of England bearer bonds, Marissa!" He rapidly counted fifteen bonds, each stating a value of one thousand pounds sterling. "Fifteen thousand pounds here, Marissa. Negotiable on the spot. Easier to conceal than cash and portable. She could have walked right out with them on her person."

"Mercy. I had hoped she did not steal from you. Too bad of her, too bad."

"Well, I am happy. They did not fleece me."

She glanced at the floor. "Yes. I understand."

"Well, then?" he demanded.

"It is just very sad. She must have had theft in mind from the beginning and had you turned out to that end. If the money is a comfort—"

"Damn it all, Marissa, I do not care about the money! I hated being swindled, taken for an easy target. Made a dupe."

She shook her head and smiled. "Of all the things in the world, you are definitely not a dupe, Allan."

"Oh?"

"Heavens, no. You are an extremely clever man."

He moved nearer to her. "Do you think so?"

"Oh, yes. Watch where you step. We must tell Norris about the broken mirror."

Allan looked up at the loose hanger. "Not your fault,

my dear. Old Cordelia must have moved that mirror many times, and the hanger gave way."

"What else is in the safe, Allan?"

He began to remove things. A packet of folded papers, letters tied together with string, and a lengthy, oblong wooden box. Marissa took the letters, and he opened the box. His mouth dropped open.

"What is it?" she inquired.

Allan showed her the contents. "It is an opium pipe and a tin container of opium."

Marissa gaped, once again surprised. The pipe of blackened wood, very thin and quite long, had a tiny bowl near the end. The round tin container had been painted with a gold dragon. "Opium," she whispered. "That is very dangerous."

He shut the box. "Yes, it is. It convinces the brain one is floating on a beautiful ocean, but you can sail too far away to get home again."

"Oh, my. How scary."

"What are the letters?" Allan asked.

She opened one. "This is to Cordelia, from—" She glanced at the end. "E. J." She read, finding the words lewd and openly suggestive. She handed them back to Allan.

"I cannot read these."

He did so, his face amazed. "Unbelievable. A rather coarse type of love letter, I gather." He opened another. "This is the same sort of smut." He rifled through the rest, then read carefully. "Listen to this. 'One more sennight, my love, then we shall be away. Give Eban all the smoke he can take, leave the evidence beside him, then proceed with our plan. I will meet you at our rendezvous. Bring the bonds and all else of value you can carry.'

"Think of it, Marissa! Cordelia planned to kill Eban, rob the house, and run off with this E. J."

"Do you think?"

"Yes, I do. Then she drove too fast. What an outcome, eh? The serpent lover is waiting for her somewhere, but death played an ace."

"The engraved ring did not come from Eban, then," Marissa guessed, "but very likely, this other fellow."

Allan picked it all up, the box with the pipe, the letters, the ring, and put them back in the safe. He closed the door and turned the key. Then he took Marissa's hand. "I could not have gotten through all this without you, Marissa. You have been invaluable."

"But I have done nothing."

He caressed her cheek. "You have been here, talking to me, making me see more clearly."

She gazed up at him. "Oh, I have been such a burden to you, Allan."

"No, never. Let us get out of this room. Come, we will tell Norris there is a mess here."

"What about the bonds?"

"Ho, I almost forgot them." He gathered them up. "I will put these in the estate safe. Then all will go right on, as if the Newtons were never here."

They left the desolate room and headed for the stairs. Marissa wondered what astonishing event would come next.

Norris shook his head in wonder when informed that the mirror had fallen, exposing the safe, about which he had known nothing. They went on to a large library, Marissa impressed by the shelves and shelves of books. There, Allan moved to a portrait of a stern-looking bearded man. He wore the clothing of a distant day and had been mounted on hinges. This swung aside to reveal a much larger safe than the one upstairs. Allan took a key from his pocket and opened it. The door made no sound.

Marissa saw the space crowded with ledgers, folders, and boxes of all sizes. Allan sorted, moved things aside, and wedged in the bonds along with the key on a cord. Then he shut the door with a click, swung back the portrait, and grinned, his expression jubilant.

"Who is that gentleman in the portrait, Allan?" she asked, regarding it.

"No one knows his name, if he ever existed. Installed with the safe, in my great-grandfather's time. No one cared to sacrifice a kinsman to hinges."

They laughed gaily.

"Now," he said cheerfully, "go and ring for Mina, and see if she will help us. Then we will be off for London, once we rid ourselves of our watcher."

Marissa darted away to do so.

****

Allan set about arranging things for the trip, spoke to Cook, and listened to kitchen gossip. He informed Norris that they were leaving under cover, at which news the butler grinned like a conspirator. The carriage and team had been prepared but would remain in the stable until called for. The gig ready to go, a groom stood by to drive.

Time sped along. Allan packed necessities and took his portmanteau to the foyer. He waited and waited. At last, Marissa and the maid, Mina, tripped down the stairs and were something to see. Mina had dressed not in her usual garb, but in the sage-green gown Marissa had worn before. Her hair had been covered not only with a scarf tied under her chin, but also a broad hat. The women were about the same height. If Mina kept her head down, they would make it.

Marissa lugged her usual valise, the poor child. Allan admired her strength. No matter what went on, she lived up to the demands. He adored every particle of her.

"Very good, ladies. The gig awaits, Mina, with Sully driving."

"Yes, my lord, we saw it arrive. I know Sully, and he knows the way to my parent's farm. I have no worries, sir." She smiled. "And I will have an extra day off."

"Well deserved, Mina. Carry on."

The maid stepped out the door, respectfully held open by Norris, stepped up into the gig, and Sully snapped the reins. The horse pulled them forward and away up the drive at a brisk pace. Mina held onto her hat in a light breeze, further hiding her face. They had almost slipped from view when out of the trees rode one of the toughs, who idly began to follow the gig on horseback, taking his time.

"There we are, Marissa. Norris, send a footman for the carriage, and we will be gone."

Norris went to do so. Allan burned with high energy. The carriage rattled to the front, the team stamping. Will jumped down, came to the door, and took the baggage. Allan rushed Marissa to the carriage, and they crowded in. The door closed, the carriage turned, the horses strained as Griggs shouted commands, and they took off up the drive.

Allan gazed cautiously at the trees and bushes but saw no one else. They cleared the gates and turned onto the road. He relaxed and studied Marissa. She sat there, tranquil, contained, a true lady. It soothed his soul.

Although elegant in her blue carriage dress, she deserved better—the best, in fact. Fashionable gowns, furs, and his mother's pearls. Then she would shine even brighter. Allan could not wait to see it.

Marissa held onto a leather strap as the carriage sped along. Soon she became certain that going so fast might tear the entire vehicle apart and fling them all into the verge crowded with yellow-flowered gorse. However, on they raced like the devil himself ran after them.

The landscape flew by, unrolling in the opposite direction they had come only yesterday. She saw the backs of things she had seen the front of then. And an awful lot had happened in between. She gazed at him, his soft felt hat, his broad shoulders and long legs. Allan had called her darling. It did not signify anything; they were friends. And the mirror breaking had been a serious danger. Still, the endearment had been lovely to hear. Not a soul had ever called her that.

Allan seemed deep in thought, so Marissa said nothing. Mercy, he must be weary of her attached to him like a barnacle to a boat. He would surely like to see the last of her. Such a humiliating situation; she would stand no more of it and must say so.

"Allan, when we get back to London, I will cash my blasted draft, and you will be rid of me."

"Is that so?" he drawled.

"I know you are tired of dragging me about, with Shaw and his ruffians on my heels. This cannot go on."

He just smiled, but it would not do.

"With sufficient money," she continued, "I can readily find somewhere respectable to stay, just for tonight, then seek out my aunt tomorrow. And you will be free. I am so thankful—"

"Hush. We are about to reach the Crescent Inn." He came to sit beside her and faced out the window. "Duck down."

"Pardon?"

He pushed her down by the back of her neck, her cheek pressed against his thigh, her hat going awry. The white flower sagged into her nose.

Marissa, immediately furious, struggled. "Let me up! Let. Me. Up!"

Allan let go, and she righted herself. "Too insulting, sir. How dare you."

"Tra la. The second man waited right beside the road, looking for your delightful self. I told you to duck."

"Oh! He saw us?"

"No, he only saw me."

She tried to adjust her hat. "You might have given me some warning." She sat up, crossed her eyes to look up, and complained, "My flower is bent."

"I do apologize. They are not after us yet. They have to assemble themselves, get their carriage, and so on. Wait for that other fellow to return. We will keep up this pace and escape them."

Marissa took off her hat and pressed the flower into place, tucking in the bent stem as well as she could.

"I will buy you a new hat," Allan offered.

She pinned it back on. "No need. This will do. As I began to say—"

"Yes," he muttered. "We need a secure place for you tonight. One your bloodhounds cannot sniff out."

She confidently said, "If I have my money, I will find somewhere to hide."

Allan waved his hand dismissively. "You cannot cash your draft today. It is Sunday, the bank is closed."

Marissa began to feel frantic. "I will sign the draft over to you, Allan, and you can give me the five hundred pounds. Or whatever you can spare."

"I am not the bank. I have taken you on, Marissa, and you are my responsibility. At least until tomorrow, then lo, the aunt will materialize, complete with vocal feline."

The carriage lurched over a series of ruts, tossing Marissa around the seat. Allan took her in his arms until the road leveled out again, more or less. All her bones began to ache from being shaken in this box like a stone. Still, the carriage flew on without let up. She found it easier to bear with Allan to hold onto.

Marissa felt a mix of emotions. In Allan's embrace, time seemed to slow, and all seemed well. Then, when she considered how far out on a limb she had climbed, it became hard not to be afraid. Ludlow would find her, present papers showing that he owned her, and Allan would be obliged to step aside. No more the cunning gambler, now the Earl of—she could not recall the name—he must guard his reputation.

Gradually, they slowed. Allan glanced out the window.

"We are nearing the outskirts of the city, Marissa. I know it has been a rough ride. Now we can be more sedate, join the traffic, and be anonymous."

"Good."

"I am confident we were not followed. Therefore, I have directed Griggs to take us to Mivart's Hotel. This is the finest establishment in London, and perfectly reputable."

"A *hotel*?" she breathed.

"Royalty stops there; the guests are from all over the

world. Perfect place for you."

Marissa did not reply and appeared stricken.

"Now what is wrong?" Allan impatiently asked.

She twisted the strings of her reticule. "I have never been to a hotel. What will they think of me?"

"That you are a paying guest," he declared. "Do not worry, I will fix it all."

She fairly cowered in the seat. "May I wait outside in the carriage while you do so?"

"Marissa—"

"If anyone ever finds out I went to a *hotel*," she fretted, "in broad daylight, with not even a maid, I will be disgraced."

"No one will find out," Allan asserted. "I will give a false name."

"Oh, gosh!" she complained. "That will complete the shame. In a hotel, with a man, under a false name."

"I did not say I would stay, Marissa. This accommodation will be for you."

Her hazel eyes widened alarmingly. "You mean, I will be—alone?"

Allan tried to reason with her. "If I stay, that is even worse. I cannot take you back to Dover Street since that may be the first place Shaw will look, regardless of Murray. I am rather out of options, my dear."

She leaned back, seeming defeated. "At this point, why should I care? My reputation is in permanent rags. I am a runaway. My father does not want me. I have no friends." Her rosy lower lip trembled. "Disgraced, I will wind up a washerwoman."

Allan quickly adjusted. "No, you will not, Marissa. Very well. I will register us as man and wife, request a suite of rooms so we do not collide in hallways, and have done with this. I will have one chamber, all very private, and you will have another. Doors will lock. Therefore. It will scarcely be any different from last night and the night before."

He would convince her. "We can order room service, and they will bring meals, whatever we like. Buck up, Marissa. Many would love to stay at Mivart's with such an engaging fellow as myself." He waggled his eyebrows.

Marissa briefly resisted, then accepted the idea. "Well. That sounds agreeable. Thank you for troubling." She studied him. "How many ladies have you taken to hotels?"

"You will be the first."

At this, she looked happy.

"I generally went to their place," he added.

Her smile dimmed. "Of course, I should not ask." She traced a fold in the upholstery with one finger. "Did you love any of them?"

"I thought you were not going to ask."

"It is difficult to resist. You have stories you could tell. I have been no place and know practically nothing. You are a storehouse of information and have lived an exciting life."

"Hmmm. Some of it got exciting, I will admit. Too exciting. I have never loved any women, Marissa. I did not have time."

She smiled brilliantly again. How quickly her mood could alter. It made him unsteady.

"Now that can change, Allan. Then again, how much time would it take to love someone, I wonder?"

He frowned. "Until you fell on your face. Love is just another gamble. As you said, it creates losers."

"Rubbish, Allan. I cannot believe you think that. I will take that particular gamble, if it comes my way. If I am lucky."

"You said you have no luck," he recalled.

"Did I? I may revise that theory. After all, look at these last three days. I met you, certainly fortunate, and you saved me from the distinct lack of an aunt. You rescued me. I have been all over the country with you, and Shaw has not laid a hand on me."

Her expression became firm. "I will not go back, and the duke will be thwarted. Father will dig deeper until the house collapses, but I will not be there. I may indeed be peppered with luck. Life will go on."

Nothing would deter this woman, Allan decided.

She peered out the window, again fascinated by the outreaches of London with its noise and stink, life being lived in the raw. Among the cluttered disarray, Marissa sat erect, her back straight, her face open to all she saw.

Allan would stay with her, all right; it had caused him sharp pains to think of leaving her. Or, even worse, of her leaving him. What a bind he had gotten himself into, and he could see no way out again.

How ridiculous, Allan grumbled to himself. The girl had a hold on him. Had pierced his careful armor and made him care, of all damn things.

The carriage made its way through traffic, turned, and turned again, and in a short time, pulled up at the busy corner of Brook Street and Davies, and the magnificent Mivart's Hotel.

Chapter Seven

Marissa's jaw nearly fell out of her head. The enormous building towered to the sky in tall stories, dominating the corner of the wide street. Grooms clad in red-and-gold livery trotted to hold the horses, the animals busily blowing air and shaking their harnesses after a long run. A doorman, imposing in his red uniform festooned with gold braid, stepped to the carriage door and opened it. He saluted, touching his tall hat. "Welcome to Mivart's Hotel."

Allan hopped out and lifted his hand to her. "Come, darling."

Her heart in her throat, Marissa stepped down.

The doorman bowed. "We are here to show you every consideration, sir."

"Thank you," Allan replied. "Griggs," he called to the coachman, "take a place in the mews stable block." He tossed him a purse of coins. "You and Will enjoy the day. I will speak to you in the morning."

"Thank you, my lord."

"Thank you, sir."

The doorman took note of Allan's title. "Would you step inside, my lord and lady?"

He held a heavy glass door wide. "The check-in desk is across to the right, sir. Enjoy your stay."

Allan took her arm, and they stepped into splendor. Marissa glanced everywhere at once as they crossed a columned entrance hall, all in creamy marble. Tables and comfy-looking chairs were ranged about. Chandeliers high above filled the space with light. Allan led her to an elaborately carved counter and a natty fellow dressed to the nines.

"Good day, sir. How many I assist you?"

"I wish a suite of rooms, your best. I cannot yet say for how long. I have business pending."

"Indeed, sir." He spun around a ledger, and Allan quickly signed.

Marissa realized she held her breath. When the room wavered, she caught a few quick breaths. The place seemed beyond belief. Very tall, olive-skinned folk in white robes hurried about, speaking in a foreign language. Others wore wonderful, colorful clothing and seemed to have significant things they would soon attend to. In the cavernous space, they came and went on a tide of activity. She stood there, marveling at this other existence, which she could never have imagined.

The man at the counter touched a silver bell, the sharp sound startling her. A hefty fellow in red livery and a smart cap rushed to them. The man held out a large brass key, and the fellow took it. "The second floor and the Yellow Suite, Forbes, if you please. My lord, we are honored by your presence and hope all is to your satisfaction."

Allan nodded, again took her arm, and they followed the footman, or whatever, up a short flight of carpeted stairs and along a hallway. They reached double doors, and the man opened them to absolute luxury.

Allan spoke. "Thank you, Forbes. We would like menu cards, both for tea and dinner."

"It will be done, my lord," Forbes said, hurrying to

open a window. "This is a fine suite facing the courtyard. Very quiet, sir." He returned, and Allan handed him a coin.

"I will be back with the menus, sir. Then you may ring for service. If I may be of any aid, for tickets or periodicals, do call on me. I am Forbes and am stationed in the lobby." He bowed himself out, closing the doors.

Marissa surveyed the sunlit room, decorated in pale tones of spring. Fresh-cut flowers decorated tables scattered about on the thick, patterned rug, scenting the air. Cushioned chairs and settees covered in fine leather or figured brocade were placed about. She found it difficult to believe she could actually be there.

"Now, this will suffice, eh, Marissa?" Allan asked.

A knock at the door. Allan opened it, and the cases were brought in. He directed this latest fellow. "That one goes that way, and I will take the other." Again, Allan handed over a coin, and the footman left. Marissa sat on the edge of a chair, clutching her reticule.

Allan, his expression pleased, also sat down. "Think you will be comfortable, Marissa?"

"Oh, I cannot doubt it. This is splendid."

He gestured. "As I said, your chamber is that way, and I am wayyyy over there."

She had to smile. "I see. We can call out to each other across this sitting room."

"Only in an emergency. I am starving hungry. When did we last eat?"

"Days ago."

"What say we go downstairs to a tearoom I noticed?"

Marissa fumbled for words. "I, um, do we dare?"

"I feel we are safe. Shaw is wandering around totally

flummoxed, and not a soul in London knows you."

"But someone may remember seeing me here. People know you, Allan. What if an acquaintance hails you? How can you explain me?"

"I assure you—"

A knock at the door. Marissa had the impulse to run but shrank in the chair. Allan answered.

"The menu cards, my lord."

"Thank you, Forbes."

Back he came and took his seat. "Therefore. We can order tea or go down and partake in the glitter."

Her tension vanished with his confident good cheer. "I choose the glitter."

"Bold girl. Take off that hat, and show the world your lovely tresses."

She touched it. "Oh. I must freshen up."

Allan pointed. "That way. I shall do the same."

Marissa hastened that direction and entered a superb bedchamber. Quite spacious, the canopied bed vast, and the dressing table boasted a huge, gilt-framed mirror. She crossed the carpet and gazed at herself, swearing not to touch it. She removed her somewhat bedraggled hat, the white flower drooping sadly, and placed it on the table. Mina's hair magic had lasted very well, so just a touch tidied it. Now, a wash would be ideal.

She headed toward what must be a dressing room. There she found not only a place for clothing, but a separate bathing room! A large brass tub sat on the tiled floor. Astounded, Marissa longed to bathe. A marble-topped washstand occupied the corner, and on the counter stood a large jug of water in a cradle. Marissa pulled the fat stopper, tilted the jug, and poured some into the basin. She unwrapped a square cake of fragrant soap and washed her face and hands. She dried with a generous cotton towel and noticed a plug in the bottom of the basin.

Marissa lifted it out, and the water rapidly drained away. She hurried to look beneath for the spill and opened the door below, but the water trickled down a pipe and on somewhere. She left the room in a state of awe.

****

Allan spruced himself up. Washed, combed his hair, inspected his teeth, gargled, and brushed off his coat. Would that he had lived so well when cast out; he might have felt a lot better about himself. In his portmanteau lay the little woolen pouch. He opened it and took out the cameo, with its poignant face. He would like to give it to Marissa. She might object to its origins, but he dropped it into his waistcoat pocket. Why he should want to give it to her mystified him.

But Marissa ought to have everything her feckless papa had pilfered from her. All the indulgences a young girl might want. Having no come out must have wounded her. Those kinds of affairs were the path to friends, beaux, good times, and all the rest.

Allan had seen it go by, in its managed parade of young females. He had understood the ritual, but it had annoyed him anyway. He had seen himself all dressed up, sitting in a hopeful line, wishing some lady would look his way. Completely unbearable.

He meandered out to the sitting room. What kept the girl? Allan leaned to the vase of flowers near him; they smelled like Marissa. He had lost his reason; the strain had gotten to him. He had not had a moment to sit down and take stock. It had been a constant tear since he met her.

Abruptly, Marissa strolled out, turning his heart warmer. The colors of her hair, the way she walked, the air she carried of pleasure and peace. Allan could scarcely get his mind around it.

"What a glorious place this is, Allan. I have a whole bathing room, and the water in the basin drains right away."

"This hotel is only a few years old," he answered. "It has all the modern conveniences." They stepped into the hallway, and he locked the doors.

"Oh, have you stopped here before?" She hesitated. "With someone?"

He put the key in his coat pocket, and they strode down the hall. "Why do you persist in thinking I have a bevy of lovers?"

She raised her chin. Allan went on guard.

"Well, I ought to know if I have joined a long line."

"God above," he muttered.

"How many is a bevy?" she now wanted to know.

"A horde. A flock, a bunch."

They reached the stairs and started down. She gazed up at him. "How about one special lady?"

Would she ever stop? Allan placed his hand on his chest in a dejected manner. "Yes, long ago, someone stole my heart," he groaned, "broke it into pieces, and abandoned me. I would have given everything to have her safely mine forever."

Marissa appeared moved, her hazel eyes sympathetic. "Oh. I am so sorry."

He turned her toward the tearoom. "I think of Ingrid almost every day," he grieved. "A wonderful, kind, and loving woman. I have never met her equal. Therefore, I guard my heart."

"How awful. What happened?"

"I went to Eton, and she took another position in Yorkshire."

"Whaaat?"

"Ingrid had been my nurse."

"Ah." She sighed. "First loves are pitiless. I well remember—oh, what a pretty place this is! May we sit anywhere?"

He gazed over the pleasant tearoom. "I suppose."

"Then, there, by the windows."

They took chairs, and a waiter arrived. "Afternoon tea?" he queried, presenting a card.

Allan studied it. "Tea, of course, then the sandwich tray. And a selection of cakes. Does that suit you, darling?"

"Yes, thank you."

The waiter went away. Marissa would have liked to read the selections. "What else did they offer for tea?'

"A range of coffees, tisanes, various muffins and scones. I asked for the good stuff."

"I begin to again get the feeling I am invisible," she grumbled. "No one offered me a card."

He leaned his elbow on the table edge and rested his chin on his hand. "You are far from invisible, Marissa. Every man in this room watched you walk in. Every man in the lobby regarded you as we passed."

Alarmed, she asked, "Why? Do I look so out of place?"

Allan smiled and shook his head. "Marissa, sweetheart, you are astonishingly beautiful."

"Oh, bosh."

The tea arrived, with plates, delicate cups, glasses of

water, sandwiches, and two tiered trays of sweets and savories. The waiter poured from a heavy silver pot, placed it on the table, and departed.

Allan gobbled a sandwich. "Everyone defers to me, Marissa. It is the way society works. They consider a countess too far above them to speak to directly."

"I am not a countess," she objected.

"In Mivart's Hotel, you are. I registered as the Earl and Countess Townshend."

"Oh, you rascal," she whispered, her eyes narrow.

"Have a sandwich. It will be just like in the mail coach, you and me against the world."

It all tasted delicious, and Marissa ate all she could. The excellent tea most refreshing, she soon felt content and watched with interest as Allan demolished the trays. He had again called her darling, adding on a sweetheart. This might be for the benefit of the hotel staff, but what would they care? He did it for himself, she reckoned. Did he think her beautiful? Impossible. He flattered her, to make her feel good. Really, so very kind of him. Her heart filled with tenderness.

If he took her to her aunt's tomorrow, would she ever see him again? That would be extremely unlikely. He would go back to Rutledge Hall and oversee the crops or whatever an earl did. Marissa sorely regretted not having seen the rest of the fine house and property. The chance would never come again.

Their odd adventure would be over, and there she would be, marooned with an aunt she did not know. Said lady would likely want to send her right back home to Ewell; well, she would not go. She would cash that draft if she had to crawl to the bank.

"Had enough of all this, Marissa?"

"Yes, thank you."

He raised a hand, and the waiter brought a ticket. Allan signed with a flourish; they rose and returned to the lobby.

"Let us take a turn through the courtyard," he suggested. "I believe the entrance is this way."

They walked down a hall. Allan opened a heavy door, and they stepped outside, the air scented with honeysuckle, greenery, and roses. They walked along a gravel pathway between flower beds. In the center, a fountain splashed into a pool where large goldfish lazed, their fins slowly moving.

They circled the area, then took seats on an iron bench.

"I have something I would like to give you." He reached into his waistcoat pocket and withdrew an object, then showed it to her.

"A cameo!" she breathed. "How charming." He held it out, and Marissa took it. Exquisite, and only about an inch across. "It is very beautifully made. In fact, it is likely quite old. I have read no one is able to do such fine carving these days." She turned it over. "Oh, Allan. It is set in gold and has—" She looked closer. "I believe this is a royal crest!"

"It is."

"Where did you acquire—Allan, surely, you do not mean to give it to me? To keep?"

He shrugged. "I cannot wear it. I won it and kept it for luck. Maybe because it reminded me of someone that I had not yet encountered."

"A royal person?"

His dark, dark eyes were hypnotic. "Now we have met, I think it reminded me of you. So, I held onto it."

Marissa could scarcely absorb this thrillingly amorous statement. "I thank you and will cherish it. I have nothing to give you, when you have been so good to me."

"I will take a kiss."

Marissa laughed, and there on a bench, while the fountain plashed and twilight gathered, she kissed Allan's lips, and her heart soared, the royal cameo held tightly in her hand.

Allan sank into some form of terrifying bliss. Marissa melted into his embrace, and he felt lost and found. Her soft mouth, her eager, innocent kiss, turned him inside out and back again, all in a flash. Astonishing. He had fallen into serious danger, became his only coherent thought. She would make him her slave. He had to shed himself of her, she would be—too damned much to handle without losing his, his…The term eluded him. Then he discarded it all. Lovely Marissa had everything he had ever wanted, while hostile and alone.

"Marissa," he murmured into her glorious hair, into her fragile ear. "It is getting dark." How irrelevant. "Let us go in."

Allan took her small hand, and they strolled inside to the commotion of the busy hotel, the lobby crowded with travelers and merrymakers. Up the stairs and along the hall, Marissa quiet, his heart bumping against his ribs. Keep hold of yourself, fool. Order dinner, chat it up, then leave her be. Act honorably, if you can remember how.

He unlocked the doors, and heat rushed over his shoulders. Marissa drifted in. Allan shut the doors again and felt enclosed in a secret hideaway. They were so alone he could taste it.

Marissa filled the entire room. She walked to the windows and looked down at the courtyard. "I will remember this always, Allan. Being so high up, sitting in that private space, surrounded by flowers. And the gift of this lovely cameo."

Marissa pinned it to her breast. It gave him a shiver to see her touch herself. He dropped into a chair. She chose the settee.

"I have no jewelry. My father put my mother's things in the floor safe, he told me, but I do not know if they are still there. He may have sold them."

"A floor safe?"

"Upstairs, in the attic, in the maid's quarters. Under a panel in the floorboards. Someone installed it ages ago."

"How old is this house?" Allan asked, glad for information and to hear her speak.

"The original structure dates back to the late sixteenth century and the second Viscount Drake. We do not know much of the first one; possibly he died in one of the constant battles, and it did not get recorded. It is thought number two had been given the land by a grateful king for some reason or other. In he marched and likely drove off the peasants. He built his house, which cannot have been much at the time, just a shelter with a fireplace. That is the section of the house Father has plundered."

"Rather late to hide Norman treasure," Allan commented.

"Of course! That is why no one credited the warning and considered it a tall tale."

"Interesting. What does the warning look like?"

"Um, it is a round iron boss"—she made a circle

with her fingers—"set into the foundation. About a handspan across, with a flower in the middle. A simple flower with six petals, like a child might draw. The etched letters surrounding it say, *Bresten Anoon Deeth*."

"Middle English," Allan exclaimed. "Break, and immediate death. Impressive. Your father may be on to something."

"Oh, stop. He has wrecked eternity as far as I am concerned. And what could be there?"

"About anything. Jewels, coins; perhaps things very old that had been valued and saved by those gone before. Maybe scrolls filled with the truth of great events. Proofs that had to be secreted. Why else go to such trouble?"

"Maybe their version of a floor safe. But if you wish to hide something, why announce it with a plaque?"

"Hmmm. I can readily see how speculations might accumulate to the point your papa had to get out there and dig."

"Beware, or it will get you too, Allan. You will hurry down to Ewell with a shovel, ready to join in the destruction."

He gazed intently at her. "You were the treasure in that house, Marissa. You have run away with the valuable object of yourself."

"Not worth tuppence in the marketplace, I believe you said, Allan."

He gave her an even more penetrating glance. "You are too precious to offer for sale."

She self-consciously smoothed her hair. "Ludlow did not think so, nor did Father. Only I thought so."

"I confirm it. I would have offered ten thousand and a faithful allegiance."

"Oh, thank you so much."

He leaned forward, his hands on his knees. "Would you have accepted me, Marissa?"

"In a heartbeat. I am beginning to think of dinner."

"As am I."

"This time," she announced, "I would like to read the offerings."

Allan stood and located the dinner card. He handed it to her with a bow. "My dear," he said, "order us a feast."

Marissa read down the list with rising joy. "They have everything, Allan, and some of it is in French."

He sat down beside her and stretched out his long legs. "Tell me."

"For appetizers, foie gras on toast, oysters, *tartine de fromage*, and duck pâté."

"And?"

"Various soups, creams or broths, then sardines, filet of turbot, or shrimp. On to the entrees. *Poulet vallée d'Auge*, chicken with apples and leeks; *suprème de volaille sous cloche*, chicken baked under a cover. The kitchen must be huge!"

"Say on, I am getting hungry."

"Roast lamb and lamb chops with a cognac and mustard sauce. Veal ragout and a roasted tenderloin of beef. All this plus *salade verte* with endive, potatoes gratin, asparagus, and haricot verts. It is an education to read this menu. What shall you have, Allan?"

"Oysters, please, no soup, and the roast tenderloin. The potatoes and the haricot verts. Plus some rolls and butter."

"I must try the lamb chops. No, no, the *poulet vallée d'Auge*. And the potatoes. I love potatoes. Unless I must peel them. But wait! What about our dessert? Tarte

Tatin, that is more apples, *canelés*, those small rum cakes, and Paris-Brest. My, that is a pastry filled with Chantilly cream. Plus, a pear tart and a butter cake with cherry sauce. Can you believe all that? I would request this Paris thing, but it may be immense. Nonetheless, I will try."

"I will have the butter cake. Pull the bell cord. Someone will come, and you can give your order."

"Me?"

He grinned. "You are the lady of the house, my dear."

Marissa pulled the bell, arranging it all in her mind.

"Ask for two bottles of iced champagne, Marissa. I prefer Heidsieck."

"Two?" she asked.

"We do not wish to run out."

"Ah."

Scarcely a minute passed, and there came a knock on the doors. Marissa hurried to open them and faced a waiter. The man carried a pad of paper and a stubby pencil.

"Good evening, my lady. How may I serve you?"

Marissa tried to look the part. "Dinner for two, please."

He raised the pad, and she recited the order as he scribbled.

"Will that be any trouble?"

"No, my lady."

"Excellent. And add, please, two bottles of iced Heidsieck champagne."

"Very good. I would estimate it will be a quarter hour."

"Thank you. We look forward to our dinner."

He nodded. "We will not disappoint."

Marissa closed the door feeling as if she had negotiated a treaty and sat down again, her mouth watering in anticipation. This promised to be the most exciting time of her whole life.

Allan watched her cross the room and deal with the waiter. He had a sudden vision of them living together. It made him feel buoyant, then his mood sank. He had been around the park a number of times. Had done things he ought not have, been with low people, and had become dangerously like them. He had gotten a little bent, better face it.

But when she came and sat beside him, he felt washed clean. Jesus. How should this go? Where could it end? The only answer Allan found acceptable consisted of wooing and winning her, then taking her home. If she would have him.

This rather annoyed him. And why would she not? When he kissed her, she nearly climbed into his clothes. It about took his breath away, Marissa so present to him, so there. When he touched her, he really touched her. She did not resist; the girl had no barriers. Marissa, unafraid, opened her heart.

It frightened him to think of other men finding her. For one, that scurvy duke would never have her. Allan had to form a plan to deal with the vampire and all his henchmen but must step carefully. Find his way, sound her out. This evening, he would gauge where he stood with her.

He must not let Marissa go anywhere without him. He glanced her way. What did she think of so seriously?

"Do you suppose we should go to my aunt in the morning," she asked, "or wait until the afternoon?"

"The afternoon. Late. Bath is over one hundred miles away."

"Really? She may have started out yesterday. We can have no idea when she will arrive." She held her lovely chin with a small hand. "What a shamble I have made of things. Such a terrible lack of planning. I should have written but, unnerved, became too afraid to wait. I needed to get away quickly, before Ludlow came with his papers and his contracts. Either that, or kill myself."

"You would not have!" Allan objected.

"I considered it. What would happen to me? A cold, unhappy life with a man I detested? The thought of him coming near me—"

The idea gave Allan pains, too. "Stop. He will never lay claim to you, Marissa. Not while I live."

She gazed at him in wonder.

A knock. Saved, Allan thought, got up, and stepped to the door.

In marched a fellow rolling a table on wheels, covered in a white cloth. After him came another, carrying a large silver ice bucket. Then a fellow with a tray followed and quickly set the table with serviettes, silver, seasonings, and tulip-shaped glasses. Lastly, men arrived carrying trays with the covered dinner and dessert choices. All this was carefully arranged on the snowy table, Marissa appeared delighted.

Allan, looked, gratified as the covers were lifted to reveal a feast. The men placed chairs.

"Shall I open the wine, my lord?"

"Please. Marissa, does it all suit?"

"Yes," she answered, her face radiant. "Yes, it does."

The wine opened with a pop, they all bowed

themselves out, and the doors closed. He held her chair, and as she sat down, Allan caught her faint scent. If he could make it through the evening without falling on her like a ravenous wolf, it would be an achievement.

He filled her glass and his own, then took his seat. He raised it and toasted. "To you, Marissa, and your future."

"Oh, I hope I have one."

Does she ever, Allan thought, I will see to it; and they drank.

Marissa swallowed the wine, which glided down her throat like hoarfrost. Allan tipped the oysters into his mouth and swallowed. She did not like the squishy look of them.

"What do they taste like?" she inquired.

"The salty sea." He proceeded to eat them all.

She ate slowly, to thoroughly taste everything. The chicken had been cooked in Calvados, an apple brandy; she could smell it. Flavorful onions and mushrooms surrounded it, the potatoes gratin a poem. Allan poured more champagne, and she drank, the wine mingling with and accenting the flavors of the food. It all tasted luscious, and she ate, having a grand time.

Allan devoured the juicy-looking beef like he had been famished, then marched through the rest of his dinner. His obvious enjoyment made her happy.

They worked their way through the meal in a leisurely fashion, but soon enough, it disappeared. The bottle of wine went empty. Allan expertly opened the second bottle, poured, and Marissa felt very relaxed. Now, they came to the dessert.

Allan emptied the container of cherry sauce over the round cake, and Marissa considered the Paris-Brest, a curve of layered pastry filled with thickened, sweet cream and dusted with milled sugar. They each tried what they had and promptly ate. She drank more champagne, her mood uplifted, her troubles distant.

"An excellent meal, Allan. Thank you. For all of this. For doing so much for me." Hot tears came to her eyes, and she blinked. "Sorry. It must be the wine."

He stood. "Come and sit down. I will get rid of all this."

She snuffled, got up, and wobbled to the settee, her legs strangely tired. Allan rolled the table, dishes and all, to the doors and put it into the hall. Marissa thought this quite efficient. Nothing for her to wash. Back he came and sat close beside her. She had never felt so mellow.

Allan's arm went around her shoulders quite easily, and she leaned against him. Marissa's thoughts spiraled crazily. Seized by a flurry of uncontrolled emotions, she abruptly knew she had gotten into terrible trouble. In the space of three hectic days, she had unwisely fallen madly in love with her champion, Allan Rutledge, Earl of—whatever-he-said. If he found out, he would run for the hills. Definitely not the sort of man who would choose to take her on permanently. Why would he?

Marissa would never inquire if he liked her. In that way. That would be hideously degrading. Crushing, if he laughed and said no, thank you very much.

With him until tomorrow, and another night between to reckon with. It would be unthinkable to let Allan just ramble off, with a tip of his felt hat. That would be foolish. A snag occurred to her; where would she tell her aunt she had been since Friday morning? Come to think of it, would she even be asked? Marissa had not seen the woman since her mother died. Had trouble remembering her face, since she had never come back, written, or anything. Another of her batty ideas, riddled with holes.

Marissa remembered—Townshend. Allan had become the Earl Townshend. Right there, a serious disadvantage. He would look higher than a country viscount's penniless daughter. Mercy! She must stop thinking these things, it felt debilitating.

"Do you want to go to your aunt's?" Allan abruptly asked.

She brushed away her worries. "Well, any port in a storm."

He studied her face. "You could stay with me."

Marissa sagged, covered in remorse. "Oh, Allan. I cannot take another thing from you. As it is, I am ever in your debt. I know you long to get back to your home and take over the estate. I have kept you running back and forth for days, with the horrid Shaw after me. It has all been outrageous."

"It has all been an adventure."

"A big gamble that I can get away from them. My last card to play will be the fact I will have been gone from home for three days and nights and am likely considered hopelessly ruined. In Ewell, at least. Maybe I should let the duke catch up with me, then tell him that."

"I doubt he would care. He might challenge me to a duel," Allan mused, "for stealing your affections."

"Certainly, he will not. I would never mention your name."

Allan shook his dark head languidly. "Shaw knows me now, and he will talk. No telling what Murray did to the man."

Horrible to imagine. "Do not bring poor Murray into

this!" she cried.

"Well, let us talk of something else. Have I told you your eyes have flecks of green and gold?"

She leaned away. "Noooo."

"Well, they do. And your hair is spun gold among the red strands. I have begun to think constantly of your breasts."

Her mouth dropped open. She shut it. "Shame on you to tease me!"

"It is the honest truth. How many other cards do you have to play?"

"Just the one."

"I wager an ace of hearts. Meaning you have come to care for me."

Allan, the rogue, liked a joke. She would play along. "Oh, good sir," she said, putting her hand to her throat and fluttering her lashes. "Surely you jest."

"No, I do not jest." Allan crowded closer; his dark eyes fixed on her. "Would you kiss me, Marissa? And consider me as a lover?"

Shock traveled through her like icy water. Had the scoundrel brought her to this hotel, a possible nest of immorality, to make a harlot of her? She gathered her poise; he would not get the better of her. Marissa lifted her chin.

"I must say, kissing you is becoming—even though I have recklessly come here, Allan, I will not, cannot, be your plaything."

He laughed, a threatening rumble. "I never thought you would, an upstanding girl like you. I like to kiss you and touch you, and it occurs to me we could work something out."

What? What? Marissa wordlessly gawked at him.

Chapter Eight

Allan took stock. Damn, he had approached her all wrong. He tried again. "Let me be plain. I like having you around. To talk to and to look at."

"Buy that parrot you mentioned," she suggested, with a small frown. "They can talk and live a long time."

"Sassy girl. I do not appeal to you? My nose is too big? My eyes do not match?"

She crossed her arms. "You are a handsome man, Allan. Your face is right off a Roman coin. As you well know."

"It is nice to be told. Am I tarnished from my sojourn in those gambling hells? Have I sunk too low for a haughty woman like you?"

"I am not haughty."

"You walk around like royalty, Marissa. You may have been burdened by kitchen chores and so forth these last few years, but you did not start out there. You obviously had a fine mother, were well brought up, and are a lady to your bones. Therefore."

"Therefore what?" she impatiently asked.

"I cannot treat you as anything less." He sighed. "So, what shall we do?"

"Pardon?"

"About the fact that for the last three days and two nights, I have been building up a huge yearning for you. I mean *all* of you, such that I cannot go on as we have."

She appeared insulted. "Well. Tomorrow I will be gone."

"That is the point. I do not want you to go to your aunt or anywhere else, without me."

A long look at him ensued. Allan assumed an air of innocence.

"I do not understand," she murmured. "Whatever are you saying?"

"That I have become infatuated. Besotted. Confounded by a great longing to hold and kiss you and take all your comforts. Of which, I imagine you have many, including your fine mind."

Allan watched her process what he said.

She leaned back to him. "Is all this the result of our propinquity?"

He grinned, triumphant. "There you are, Marissa. Only you would know the term propinquity. You have stolen my heart, girl." Allan had enough of this roundabout chatter. "Cards on the table and my fortune in your hands. I have fallen wildly in love with you, Marissa Barrington, runaway princess."

Having nothing else to convince her, Allan took her in his arms. Gazed into her face and kissed her lips with fervor and passion, his life on the line. And promptly tumbled off a cliff. Fiery tendrils wove around him, and he swiftly became a conqueror. Generations of ruthless ancestors, who had generally slashed their way to good fortune under one avaricious king or another, called to him. *Take what you want*, they whispered, and Allan obeyed. He set out to seduce her, possess her, so she could never leave him. Would never want to. Marissa would belong to him.

He put his arm beneath her knees and scooped her

onto his lap, relishing her slight weight.

Her hazel eyes sparkled in the lamplight; her cheeks pinked, but she said nothing. The gambler in him judged the signs. She looked alarmed, and this made her all the more tempting. She radiated sex, but to his practiced appraisal, she did not know this.

Would he be a swine to touch this innocent? Yes. Should he stop? Not yet.

"Could you love me, Marissa?" he whispered in her ear. He kissed her some more, felt her soften and accept him. "Belong to me in every way?"

Still, she said nothing. He began to pull the pins from her hair, and it fell onto her shoulders and his arm in a shining cascade, almost as if she were naked before him. Allan bought a handful to his nose and inhaled her scent, taken by a sensation of utter and complete worship. Marissa, an angel, had descended from heaven, chaste and pure; how could he even imagine—

"What ways are those?" she breathlessly asked.

He snapped back to reality and let her go. "I had in mind…forget it. I got carried away."

"Oh, Allan," she pouted. "You put your armor back on. To prevent the dreaded cuddles."

"And well I might!" he almost yelled in frustration. "Do you know where this could lead?"

She pushed her hair away. "For a moment there, I had some hope. Then you remembered to be angry and defensive."

Allan gritted his teeth, planned numerous ways to thrash her, and wished he had a drink. The champagne had never touched him. He longed to get out of these confining rooms and collect his wits.

"How about going downstairs for a coffee?" he

asked.

She shook her head. "I am too full." She paused. "What I would love to do is have a bath."

This set off lurid images in his mind of Marissa wet and naked. "Pull the bell cord, and it shall be done."

"May I?"

"Certainly. While you do that, I will step downstairs. Is that agreeable?"

"Yes, thank you."

Allan hustled out the door as if the furies were nipping at him, closed, and locked it. In the hallway, he breathed deeply. He had almost made some kind of blasted commitment, but he had escaped. He hurried down the stairs and across the crowded lobby, people swirling all around him. Armor? Angry and defensive? What the hell had she been talking about?

****

Marissa proceeded to pull the bell cord, then waited. In moments, she answered the knock. A footman nodded politely.

"Good evening, my lady."

Maybe they called every woman that. "Good evening. I would like to request a bath. Can that be done?"

"Yes, ma'am. The maid will enter from the bedchamber door and should arrive shortly."

Marissa gestured. "That way is my room. Thank you."

She shut the door, walked to the bedroom, and to another door she had not noticed, leading to the hall. She sat down at the dressing table and regarded her reflection. Allan, that slippery eel, had nearly spoken actual words while romancing her. Then she had asked him a question, which she had found to be an error. He instantly reverted to the gambler and decided the wager had grown too big. He had the cards, she suspected, yes, he did, but feared to play them. Feared to lose, feared she would hurt him. The poor dear had become tangled, caught in his own nets.

A tap at the service door. She answered it to face a maid and a footman. A cart on wheels stood between them, large ewers aboard. Steam wafted up.

"Ma'am," he said and rolled in, followed by the maid, who curtsied politely.

"My lady, I am Sally, come to give you any needed assistance."

Gosh. "Lovely."

The footman went on to the bathing room, and she heard the splash of water. Soon, he returned and, without a word, pushed the cart out the door again, and it closed.

"How may I assist you?" the maid inquired.

"If you would unfasten this gown, I will be all right. My maid is not with me," she said with some embarrassment.

"Many ladies do not travel with a maid," the girl said, unfastening buttons, "but depend on hotel services."

Marissa, consoled, relaxed. "I never stayed in a hotel before. Certainly not one so grand as Mivart's. I like it very much."

"It is hailed by all as the best accommodation in London. I will prepare the bathing room." The maid strolled away.

Marissa opened the valise, shed her clothes, and found her robe. In the bathing room, the maid had prepared soap and towels. The robe taken, Marissa sank into the luxury of the excellent tub, the very warm water heavenly. All her kinks and muscle tensions soaked away.

"Did you wish your hair washed?" Sally asked.

"No, it is a world of trouble to dry. I will put that off until next time."

Handed a sponge, Marissa washed with soap that smelled very fresh, like mint. When Allan came back, she would have a few things to say. He must not continue to hold out affection, then when she reached for him, take it away. It had become exasperating. Meantime, this bath removed all sorts of bruises, and she sat back, quite at her ease.

****

Allan sauntered a few blocks down Brook Street until he came to a pub. Went in, stood at the bar, and sipped a large whiskey, which solved nothing. He had to decide about Marissa, but doing so would be full of pitfalls. Could his turmoil and indecision be real, could it be actual, this overwhelming need to have Marissa for always? After a mere three days? Or had he just begun to recover from being lost in the dark, in an interrupted life? Had it made him heedless?

He glanced around the room, wreathed in cigar smoke and filled with men. Men alone. Men with nowhere else to go. No gentle creature waited for them.

Allan had no decision to make, that had been decided somewhere on the road. He powerfully wanted Marissa with him. As they had been these last few days, racketing around the country. Everything had rather swamped him, including her unpredictable, nosy assumptions. Or, true to form, he had hesitated, hedging his bet, ever alert. Not willing to chance an unnecessary gamble and possibly a painful loss. Plus, his edges were a bit soiled here and there. The stench of that inn still hung on him. He had become the one that needed a bath. Allan emptied the glass.

Jesus. He imagined Marissa in the tub, bathing right this minute. Wet and sleek, her glorious hair all piled up, dripping water on her skin with a—

"Another, sir?" the barman queried.

"No," he said. "I have somewhere important to be." Allan paid and left, all expectation. When she got out of the bath, he could kiss her and smell her freshness. Talk to her, tell her how he felt. He quickly retraced his steps, the showy doorman bid him good evening, and he headed for the stairs.

Allan's heart jumped in alarm. He sat down in the nearest chair, picked up a copy of the Sunday *Times*, held it in front of him, and peeped around the edge. He might be mistaken, that night last year had gone fuzzy. He gazed intently at the tall, slim man at the desk. Around thirty-five or so, he carried himself rigidly, all the while cautiously checking his surroundings. A man with him talked steadily. The clerk smiled in an obsequious way, and a fellow rushed to serve him. The man turned his way, and Allan hid behind the paper.

Him, no doubt of it; Allan held up the *Times*, positive. The bloody Duke of Ludlow had just checked in.

The two of them went up the stairs. Why the blazes had the man come to London? Could it be because— Allan opened the paper further and found notices of engagements. And saw Stubbins had come through. He read the prominent type.

The engagement of The Honorable Marissa

Barrington to Lord Allan Rutledge, Earl Townshend, is hereby formally announced.

Amazingly, he had laid the groundwork before he knew his own mind. The duke might have seen the notice and come running. Therefore, Allan must be stealthy. He folded the paper, stood, tucked it under his arm, and strolled to the desk. The man happily greeted him.

"Yes, my lord, how may I help?"

"Did I not just see the Duke of Ludlow checking in?"

"Yes, sir, indeed you did."

"Hmmm. I did not expect him until tomorrow. Is he on the second floor with us?"

The man, obviously reluctant to give out information, answered, "Uh, no, my lord. His Grace is staying on one of the higher floors."

Allan would find the fool. "Excellent. Nothing will be amiss. One more thing. Is there a clergyman available in the hotel?"

"Yes, my lord. The chapel is just down the hallway from the stairs. Reverend Woolsey will be there from eleven until two tomorrow, or by appointment."

"Very good. Thank you."

"Any time, sir."

Allan hastened to the stairs and up, trotted down the hall, and swiftly went in the doors. The duke had arrived too late by half. Marissa would belong only to him.

****

After the bath, she donned her nightie and robe. Sally stayed, kind enough to take down and brush Marissa's hair.

"Such a wonderful color, my lady, all red and gold. Very glossy and thick, too."

"Thank you." She heard the doors to the sitting room open and close. Allan had returned.

The maid replaced Marissa's brush on the table. "There you are. Shall I braid it?"

"Please. Here is my ribbon." Marissa wanted to look nice for Allan, the scamp, and adjusted the thin robe. Maybe she should not go out in this state of undress. On the other hand...

Basically, she would like to give Allan a shove for being so standoffish and also for coming too close. For hinting at things, then not following through. He kissed her passionately, got her all worked up, then he turned away! He gave her heated looks she could not interpret. Too unfair. She would tell him—

The maid tied the ribbon and stepped back. "Then I will leave you, if you need nothing else."

Marissa rose, went to her reticule, withdrew three of her precious shillings, and handed them to the maid. "Thank you, Sally."

"Good night, my lady." The maid curtsied and left.

She smoothed her hair and pinched her cheeks. A knock at the other door. "Yes?"

"Are you coming out, Marissa?" Allan inquired.

Maybe he should come in, she grumbled, went to the door, and opened it. There he stood, looking worried, then relieved.

"A *braid*," he whispered, swept her into his arms and kissed her lips like the end of the world had come.

Despite her best intentions and determination to fully speak her mind, Marissa sank under his spell without a qualm. What did it matter that Allan could be cranky and guarded himself? She put her arms around his neck and kissed him with good energy. He twirled her around, and her feet left the floor; he whirled her back to the settee and plopped her on his lap.

"You smell like a garden, Marissa. By God, you have no clothes on."

She caught her breath.

"I adore you, girl, and think you appreciate my worth. Therefore, how about marrying me?"

Another of his jokes. It annoyed her. "What is this, Allan?"

"I am proposing. I intend to secure a special license tomorrow, and we can marry before the day is out."

Had he gone daft? Marissa gave him a push. "Ludicrous. You cannot wish to marry me; I am practically a stranger!"

"To my surprise, I do. It came on me of a sudden that without you, my life would be sterile and empty."

Suspicious, she inhaled. "Ah. You have been drinking, Allan, and do not realize what you are saying."

"I can handle my liquor. I mean every word. We could have a grand time together, as we have these last days. That is, if you care for me. Which you do, I am convinced. Your kiss says so. The feel of you in my arms and on my lap confirms it. I now think I became yours from the first." He looked around for the *Times*, which he sat on. He juggled Marissa and retrieved it, opened it to the page, and pointed.

Marissa took it and read, then gasped. "Who did this? We have only just met!"

"Yes, I know. I told Stubbins to put the notice in the Sunday paper, to ward off Ludlow. And because I had the impulse to make a claim on you. Although that had not yet come clear to me."

"Well, but to allege we are engaged—I mean, how

will you recover from this? It will make a scandal. No one will believe you sincere if later you meet—"

"They will believe whatever we tell them. We are affianced to the world, and when we marry, the duke will retire from the field, solidly defeated."

Marissa stared, thoroughly muddled.

Allan kept his head, swamped by a tide of affection for this innocent lamb. Not only did she have no designs on him or his title, she seemed genuinely startled by his offer. She thought it over, her expression solemn. He waited.

"No, Allan. It is very kind and generous of you, but I will manage. I have escaped my father, and no one else can make me marry the duke, contracts or no. Ludlow cannot just carry me off, and surely, no vicar would consent to marry a weeping and unwilling bride. Unless paid to do so," she amended. "But it is useless to consider that. In fact, the dunderhead has likely given up on me, since I have fled Surrey with another man. I will be free to make my own way and will hear no more of him."

Stubborn girl. "Well, that is what you think. Allow me to reveal—"

"Not to mention the fact," she went on, "that you must marry well, with heirs to consider. After this escapade, I am not socially up to that."

"Bloody society means nothing to me!" he yelped.

"But it will follow you and your children," she insisted. "If your wife is unsuitable, they will suffer."

"Where do you dig up this nonsense, Marissa? My title will be sufficient, believe me, to cover any social sins; as if either of us cares. And how about the fact that I have been a rather well-known, high-stakes gambler for some time? Dawdling about in rough situations, with rougher folks. Eh? Let my heirs deal with that. We are both notorious according to society's rules and likely, the righteous citizens of Ewell as well. I do not give a damn, and neither should you."

Marissa studied him. Allan labored to appear sincere.

"What has happened to all of a sudden change our course, Allan? This is not your usual devil-may-care attitude."

He held her closer. "You have not known me long enough to establish norms," he objected. "I worship and adore you, Marissa, and crave a thousand kisses."

"Do you, now? I know that I have them." She regarded him carefully. "First say what happened when you left. You went somewhere for a glass and came back quite changed."

"I did, longing to have a drink and groom my wits, unable to decide what to do about you, about us. When I got to the pub, I found it filled to the doors with bad air and depressing men. I drank that glass and thought of you in your bath, all wet and sudsy. I realized how much I never wanted you to go away and rushed right back here to say so."

Her hazel eyes were on him. "And?"

Might as well tell her. "Coming across the lobby, to my astonishment, I saw Ludlow checking in."

She started in surprise. Allan held on.

"He did not see me, but I believe he saw the *Times* notice," Allan said cheerfully, "and has come to kill me."

"Horrors! Does he somehow know we are here?"

"Not likely; this is just the best hotel in town. I wish to stop the blockhead from pursuing you, so let us cement our relationship."

"Just a moment!" she protested. "Do you mean you *know* Ludlow?"

"Not exactly. About a year ago, I lightened his purse by a thousand pounds that he became most unhappy to lose. He considered himself a master player, and I tripped him up. The light was low; he will not remember me."

"Oh, yes, he will! I will leave at dawn," she announced. "He will never know I came here and will not do anything untoward. Like shoot you. Which, of course, he will not."

Allan gave her a squeeze. "Not a chance, Marissa. You will not leave my side until I obtain that license in the morning. Then, between eleven and two tomorrow, a respectable reverend is available in the hotel chapel."

"A chapel? Here? How do you know this?"

"I asked at the desk."

Marissa jumped right to her bare feet. "God in heaven," she cried, "you registered us in your name, Lord Whosit and wife!"

"That is Townshend," he drily corrected. "With an h."

She paced around. "Ludlow will find out. You do not know how devious he is. He has underlings like Shaw everywhere and has found us. Maybe someone right in this hotel has informed him! I tell you, Allan, he knows we are here. You should leave immediately; I can hold him off."

He tugged at her sleeve. "You should sit back down."

She pulled the silk robe closer, but Allan had seen her delicious shapes and curves. She stood there proudly, so virginal, so untutored in seduction, sex lay all over her

166

in ruffles. It made his heart thump with want.

Marissa perched on the edge of the seat. "I have some difficulty with your, ah, suggestion, Allan. You kiss me ardently, and we have had several, um, exchanges of feelings. I begin to think you may care for me, then when I become—involved, you turn away. This is unnerving. So, if we are engaged, at least in the *Times*, will you not? Turn away?"

The darling! "Marissa, I have had to exercise severe control since we met, to not lose what is left of my honor and seize you every moment we are alone. So, I have tried to keep sane, though sorely tempted."

She tilted her head. He wanted to bite her thick braid.

"Even in the mail coach?" she inquired.

"Absolutely. Even before the sandwiches."

A small silence formed. Allan got worried, then she whispered, so low he almost did not hear.

"I do not wish you to turn away, Allan. Ever."

His blood thundered through his veins and shook him. "I am your servant," Allan answered and meant it with his entire being.

Every daring, rebellious notion Marissa had ever considered clamored for attention and urged her on. Her first thought: make him yours, give him so much he will never turn away again. The second involved finally getting some genuine loving and sensual passion for herself. No more wondering and waiting, with no knight coming to court her and nothing to assuage buried longings considered improper. Why not take the ultimate gamble? With him.

Allan had no rules, he said so, and would show her all she wanted to know and experience. Anyway, fascinated by his male power, his sheltered heart, Marissa tenderly loved all of him. And she wanted more kisses, more words and touches, now, tonight. She must speak, before the moment wasted away. The words were right there, ready to be said.

"Let us go to your room, Allan."

He hopped up. "Are you sure, Marissa?"

"Oh, yes. I am." She stood and began to turn down the lamps. He hovered behind her as she did so, put his arm around her, and they strolled that way. Marissa marshalled her courage.

Allan opened the door, the room a mirror image of hers. His portmanteau stood open on a table. Lamps shone, banishing shadows, the bed untouched. He took off his coat, as Marissa shyly observed. In his white linen shirt, he seemed bigger. Her heart bumped; her breath came short. What a demented idea! She would make an excuse and hurry out the door.

But it had become far too late for caution. His gaze piercing, he pulled the shirt out of his breeches and took it over his head. Marissa gaped as he tossed it aside. Allan, an immense god in tantalizing flesh, stood before her. She smelled a faint cologne. Her mouth went dry.

"Is this too much?" he quietly asked. "Change your mind?"

She answered by removing her robe and placing it on a chair. The thin cotton nightie was a farce; likely Allan could see right through it. She touched the lace panel at the bodice with a nervous hand. "No. I have not."

He sat down on the chair and took off his boots. Stood and unbuttoned his falls, as he grinned. Why, the rogue meant to tease her!

"Positive?" he crooned, stepping nearer.

"Stop this, Allan. I am not afraid to see you," she lied.

In a swift series of moves, he stripped naked and swept aside the puffy comforter. Marissa staggered against the bed, undone by the sight of him. He loomed, enormous, with wide shoulders, had a patch of dark hair on his broad chest, and seemed brown from the sun. He had those long legs, large feet, and the most colossal member she had ever envisioned in a fantasy. Combined, it all made her dizzy and faint.

Then he moved next to her, against her. He undid the ribbon and shook her braid loose. It all seemed a dream, every gesture slow and effortless, his hands on her, the feel of his skin, the scent of his hair, his strength. He took the nightie down her arms, and it fell to the floor. She stood as tall as possible and would be brave.

"Come to bed with me, beautiful Marissa; be a wife to me."

The invitation daunting, she would not turn back. Allan easily picked her up, placed her in the center of the bed, then climbed in after her. She glanced all around, to remember everything.

A shower of kisses, his arms cradling her. Little bites and licks on her skin and delicious pets and caresses. Waves of intense longings without name showered over her in sharp prickles. Her hands learned Allan, the quality of his skin, and the ways he touched her, all of it nothing like she had imagined, being with him, naked, in his bed.

He caressed her breasts lovingly, rubbed his cheek against them, took one nipple into his mouth, and gently sucked. She shut her eyes tightly. This felt *incredible* and turned her inside out with outlandish sensations. He favored them both until Marissa tensed, about to shout, then transferred his efforts to rubbing her stomach. Tender yet demanding kisses fogged her brain.

God save her, he put his hand over her pubic hair and gripped the curls. She flushed hotly all over as he reached down, nudged open her legs, and boldly parted the hidden folds. She went rigid and seemed mysteriously quite damp; he then put one long finger against her *there* and pushed a little. She gulped a breath. He pushed more, and a flash of light covered her for an instant; he moved his finger in a circle, and she died away. More kisses everywhere. He whispered in her ear.

"I will love you all over, Marissa, my angel, my darling. Inside and out. This is part of it. Relax, let me awaken you and show you how you can feel. Let yourself go. No rules, no limits, just you and me and our loving."

Remarkably, she floated in a lazy stupor and only expected pleasure. He touched a place with his thumb, rubbed, and she moaned, torn asunder. Lightning throbbed through her bones, and she shivered all over, her flesh in a tumult of thrills. She rose up, every muscle taut, vibrated in a hot wind, shivered, then went absolutely limp.

"Allan, Allan," she mumbled.

"Marissa, my love. See how you can shine like the stars? You like my loving, and precious girl, there is more, much more to learn. I will teach you everything to make all your senses dance."

Marissa hummed all over with satisfaction.

Chapter Nine

Allan could not believe his luck. He had taken the gamble Marissa would hear him and believe him. Then she had asked to be with him. Asked! Such a thing had never happened to him before. And with beauty and grace, she came into his arms and his bed. He had delighted her, he had seen it, felt her tremble and climax in his arms, the best yet ahead. A precious virgin girl, he must allow for that.

He held her close and kissed her, stroked her gorgeous hair, and caressed her incredible skin. "I love you, Marissa. I believe I have looked for you all my life."

"Oh, Allan. How dear of you to say so."

"I mean it. I never would have thought we would be here, together like this."

Her lovely smile. "You must know I love you, too. All this time. Every day."

"Noooo," he breathed. "I did not know. Tell me."

She smoothed his hair, making his scalp tingle.

"In the mail coach, we truly talked, as I have never spoken with anyone. When I met you, it made me realize how lonely I have been. And you were so dashing."

He laughed. "Dashing?"

"Oh, yes. Handsome, very masculine, and a little dangerous. Quickly lovestruck, I became so much trouble, I thought you would be extremely glad to be rid of me."

"I could not let you go, Marissa. I had to take care of you."

She snuggled in his arms, full of heat and musky smells, her glorious red-gold hair tousled on the pillow. Desire rose in him like a sun as he made love to her with kisses, nibbles, and tender bites. Her skin warmed as his mind filled with a hundred variations of desire. Allan moved over her, between her sweet knees, her pretty legs alongside him. It was ecstasy to press his cock into the fragrant wet and against her secret passage.

Marissa held him tightly as he balanced there, on the brink, holding himself back. It would be her first time, it must be right, she must be ready. She lifted her hips, and Allan, confident, carefully moved into position. When Marissa put her legs around him, he became elated. He placed himself at her gateway to paradise, begged the gods that he would not cause her pain, and pushed. The woman opened to him like a flower, and Allan slowly pressed in.

Marissa writhed, turning his brain to a jelly, and raked her nails down his arms. Allan thrust in mightily, and she cried out in pleasure. He rejoiced, withdrew partially, and drove in again, seating himself perfectly. His, his forever, and Allan could not get enough of her, his salvation, his redemption, and now, he would make her his own.

Marissa clung to Allan for her life, rapidly taken up in a maelstrom. Such a monumental thing to be engaged in, it filled her mind. She flailed through riveting environments that rumbled through her flesh. Shaken like a rug, the dust of old thoughts and ways of being blew away, every particle of her being revitalized.

When he began to slip from her, she grasped him

with every muscle. Back he came, his member a heavy shaft of tormenting enticement, to fill her again and again. A deep gratification lay just beyond her, and she reached and reached as Allan loved her. Hours passed in a blur as she strained, yearning for all he would give her.

Then it came.

A storm of liquid ripples and misty rainbows flowed through her flesh like a silvered river and filled her entire body with glory. Myriad delights scattered through her like burning rain, and she rose high and higher, peaked, then swiftly tumbled down and down again to the moment, cushioned in Allan's strong arms.

He paused; all his muscles locked. He gazed down at her, concentrated his efforts, thrust one final time, and shuddered, giving his all to her in a rapture. Marissa closed her eyes and held him. They belonged to each other now, for as long as always.

A sense almost of rebirth, of real human experience, had at last come to her, down through the ages. By a miracle, she had found it all with Allan Rutledge. He had brought a whole world to her, and she longed to live there, with him. A man she had known for three days had become vital to her existence. A chance meeting, an accident of time, had brought them together in the same place, at the same instant.

And in these busy days, Allan had changed as much as she had. In this timeless intimacy, she had glimpsed his soul. Now he was completely known to her, in all his youthful tenderness and vulnerability. Marissa valued him more than ever for what she had seen. Her dashing gambler still lingered there, and she loved him, too.

He moved aside to spare her his weight but kept her close. She reached up to caress Allan's cheek. "Thank you, for taking me to such a fabled place."

"I did not hurt you in any way, my love?" he murmured.

"No. I am obviously in the group whose hymeneal membrane is not an impediment to intercourse."

"By the gods!" he exclaimed. "I reckon you read that somewhere?"

"No, I questioned Mr. Karl, our doctor in Ewell. A German fellow from Heidelberg, he considers himself to be advanced in his thinking. I assured him I asked for a dear friend."

Allan laughed merrily.

"I had heard a few alarming and discouraging tales of marriage that I suspected were exaggerations, so I needed to find out facts. You, my sweet, are the proof that lovemaking is splendid all around."

He hugged her. "Unquestionably the pinnacle of my sexual experience, Marissa. All else was common dross. A thing of base necessity. This time with you, a panorama of exquisite coming together in love and goodness, is all clean and right."

Allan turned to her, his arms around her. "Marissa Barrington, will you do me the extreme honor of becoming my countess?"

Marissa pressed her fingers to her lips. Time seemed to rock to a halt. Here in his question, the chance of a lifetime. If Allan thought her suitable or whatever, if he loved her, why should she hold back?

"I know we have not known each other for long," he said on, "and I have a lot of annoying habits, but, well, say something."

The words rushed out. "Yes. Yes, yes. I will marry you, my Lord Townshend, tomorrow between eleven and two. If you can procure that license."

Allan rolled right over her. "Believe that I will, girl. But accept the fact that I have bedded you, and you are already my wife."

"Oh, I do not know," she lightly remarked, running her hand through his choppy hair. "Is that everything? Perhaps you had best show me again what it is to be bedded by a notorious gambler."

He nibbled her throat. "Ah ha, my pretty runaway, prepare yourself to be transported by a master."

So, Marissa, with a deep sigh, did so. And found his loving better than before.

****

Allan woke in the night and for a moment forgot his location. Then he felt the softness of Marissa's body beside him. All that had happened between them rolled over him like wagon wheels. What had he done? You primitive, he chided himself, deflowering this innocent, this tender babe. He would be struck by lightning for— half a moment! He would marry her. Today! Yes, yes, the special license must be obtained. That beggar Ludlow showing up had tipped his hand, but what the hell.

Allan allowed himself to remember the feel of her in his arms, the way his cock had slid into her in an ecstasy and fit her passage like putting on a silk glove. He had never been more enthralled, or at the last, more wholly satisfied. It had been a gigantic experience. Then it had all happened *again*. Marissa had blossomed like a field of flowers, and he had nestled in her fragrant petals, totally fulfilled. And there were other things he could do to bewitch her and himself. He would get to that.

Allan snuggled closer to her. Therefore. He must

hustle off to Doctor's Commons first thing. And take Marissa with him. Take her everywhere with him, from now on. He closed his eyes and thought of the future with her. Images paraded in his mind of happy times, and soon, with Marissa safely near, he slept again.

****

Marissa detected intense warmth and a great weight at her side. She opened her eyes, shocked to find herself—then she remembered every detail of the night, all in an extravagant procession. She had done astounding things and had allowed even more outrageous acts to be performed on her person. With a shiver, she once more felt Allan's hands, his mouth, and all the rest of him moving over and into her. To her astonishment, it had all been very natural, once she got used to him. And the things he could do to toss her around London on a cloud.

But what had she done, going this far? Allan could not be serious about the license, the chapel, and all that; he had gotten caught up in the moment. Carried away bodily.

Or had he? Perhaps—

Oh, my God, no! Allan had seen Ludlow! In this hotel. Dread moved over her like a shroud, and she pushed it away. She had made her choice, however it went. Ludlow lay in the past. She had jumped free of him and would continue to do so, Allan or no Allan. That thought gave her sharp pains in her chest. She would be strong and resilient. As a woman on her own, she would take life as it came.

That decided, Marissa made herself comfortable. Amazing how two people could fit in one bed like this. She had gotten her cuddles after all, she gloated, and he definitely did not turn away. How warm he felt. Allan would certainly be nice to sleep with in the winter. But winter seemed far away. Eons away. Marissa, safe beside her hero, relaxed, and by and by coasted away and slept.

****

Shafts of sunlight crossed the ceiling, and Allan woke. Marissa, still without a stitch on, held his hand in both of hers. Sound asleep, her lips rosy and pink, her satin skin glowed. Her loose hair formed an abundant halo of bright colors. When he had seen the braid, so youthful and virtuous, he had nearly fallen to his knees in worship of her female perfection.

I do not wish you to turn away, Marissa had said, and his heart had enlarged with expectation. And she had not turned away either, though he had seen a flurry of hesitations change her hazel eyes. Such a brave girl to trust him. Allan vowed he would never let her down.

Marissa stirred, murmured faintly, and Allan became still. She moistened her lips with the tip of her pink tongue, and his muscles went weak. Very slowly, she opened her eyes, looked at him in some surprise, then smiled. His heart twitched; she must be the most beautiful creature that had ever lived.

And before they exchanged a word, Allan knew he truly and absolutely loved Marissa Barrington and would for the rest of his life.

"Good morning, my lord," she whispered in a husky voice.

Enchanted, he said, "Good morning, my beautiful lady. Any regrets?"

"No. None. And as for everything you said, I will not hold you to any of it." She pulled the comforter closer and glanced away. "I suppose it came to extensive propinquity after all."

He hastened to correct this. "No, just you and me, at last together. If we had only known each other for an hour, my feelings for you would have been the same. I have foolishly tried to ignore them. I love you, Marissa. I say it again, as I said it last night. Now it is your turn."

She snuggled into his arm. "I do love you, Allan. Excessively. I meant it last night, and do now. I tried to give you a way out."

"Sorry. I have dealt myself in." Allan repressed a demanding erection, not wanting to be a pest. "Let us order a sumptuous breakfast," he suggested.

"Mmmm." She smoothed her hand down his chest and across his belly, jarring his brain. "We could tarry for a few minutes, could we not? I believe it is very early."

"Oh, Marissa, darling. Come here. I have things to show you."

****

Marissa floated in a haze of Allan's loving revelations. They rolled around the bed, engulfed in a passion that made her tremble with flowing, ongoing undulations. No sense of time or necessity intruded until at last, they lay quietly in a spent embrace.

"I must eat or die," Allan finally murmured.

"Yes, please."

He sat up and loomed over her menacingly. Marissa stifled a giggle.

"Get up then, lazy girl. Let us freshen up as necessary, eh? Then I will join you in the sitting room, and we will order a banquet."

"I will be quick." Marissa slid out of bed, gathering her nightie and robe as Allan regarded her with obvious interest. She breezed out the door and sauntered across the sitting room, defying the world.

She would do without that maid, found the water cradle full, if tepid, and washed with care, so excited, she fairly trembled. Finished with all that, she searched through her valise, grieving that she had brought so few clothes. She chose the pale-yellow muslin, with the yellow sash.

Marissa paused to catch her breath. It had been such an intense night; she may not have slept. She must save energy or she would not last the day, which promised to be most eventful. She began to dress, taking care to wear her best underthings. She sat at the dressing table and dealt with her hair. Marissa brushed patiently, then piled it all up on top of her head, in various curls and loops, using all her pins.

A knock at the hall door. The maid, she decided, how nice to be attended. She crossed the room, and opened the door. Something wet smacked over her face. Marissa struck out, hit a solid mass, then nothing.

****

Allan washed and shaved in record time, before he starved to death. He dressed with his usual care for his appearance, and lastly, he retrieved the woolen pouch from his portmanteau. The heavy, gold signet ring; he had kept it all this time, forbidden to wear it. Robbed of his title and everything else. On his little finger at last, he accepted the earldom and his place in it. The ring had come down the generations, and now he became one of them.

Allan donned his coat, and feeling splendid, went to the sitting room to wait for Marissa. He gazed out the window at the fine day and the courtyard below, the fountain in the center silent from here. Then he heard a door open and quickly close in Marissa's room. A sharp stab of fear struck his spine, he paused, then hurried to her door.

"Marissa?" he called. "Are you all right?"

Silly of him, Allan thought, but she did not answer. He opened the door and quickly searched through the rooms. Jesus Christ, Marissa! He bolted out the service door and looked each way. Nothing, no one.

That fucking duke! Allan slammed the door and headed for the stairs, his mind jumping. How could he find her? He trotted down them and spied Forbes, the muscular bellman, and rushed to him.

"My lord," the man said. "How may I help?"

"Forbes, I urgently need a favor."

"Anything, sir."

"The Duke of Ludlow has kidnapped my lady. I must know what rooms he occupies."

The man frowned, doubting the request.

Allan pressed a sovereign into Forbes's hand. "Help me out, Forbes, I am desperate. Come with me, and see I am being truthful. If there is trouble with the management, I will stand by you, I swear."

Forbes pocketed the coin. "This way, sir. His Grace is on four."

They hastened to a door and another set of stairs. Up they both went, Allan prepared to kill Ludlow, slowly and painfully, if he had harmed Marissa. A hot ball of murderous anger had lodged in his chest. They reached four, both of them breathing hard. Forbes beckoned, and Allan followed him to a set of double doors. The man nodded, then stood aside.

Allan, not about to knock, stepped back and rushed

the doors, putting all his weight behind it. The lock gave, and both doors crashed open. Forbes stepped forward anxiously as Allan jumped into the room, his fists raised.

Ludlow stood beside a sofa, upon which lay an inert Marissa, one arm outstretched, her fingers trailing the carpet.

"Get away from her!" Allan shouted. "What have you done?"

Ludlow smiled self-importantly. The ever-faithful Shaw raised a long-barreled pistol, and Forbes ran from the room.

"You will remain quiet, my lord," Shaw warned. "You have evaded His Grace, who only sought to claim his property."

"Is Marissa all right?" Allan insisted. "I must see that she is breathing." He stepped toward the sofa, measuring the distance, calculating his chances.

"Stay back!" Shaw demanded, coming closer and jabbing at him with the pistol. "I only gave her—"

Allan smashed his fist into Shaw's fat face and grabbed the pistol as the man fell heavily onto his back. He pointed it squarely at Ludlow's impassive, cruel face.

"I will destroy you, Townshend, for this outrage," he snarled. "The girl belongs to me. I paid for her; I own her. I have planned to have her for months, do you hear? And now she will be mine. Mine! I *always* get what I want." He snorted meanly. "I have the contract, signed and witnessed, right here." Ludlow took a step toward a table.

"Stand very still, or I will cheerfully shoot you," Allan threatened.

"You cannot," the duke replied in an insolent tone. "The pistol is empty and only a ruse."

"Like the chloroform? The place stinks of it."

The duke continued to sidle toward the table.

"I tell you one more time, I will shoot. Not to kill you, but I can see that you never walk again."

Doubt crossed his face. "You would not."

"Are you willing to take that gamble? I know for a fact you are a worthless card player. I took a thousand pounds off you at the Nightingale, only a year ago."

The duke's narrow cheeks reddened. "I know you." He grimaced. "You cheated."

"I never cheat. I outwitted you, as I have outwitted you with Marissa. She belongs to me, body and soul. After a number of days and nights alone with her, need I elaborate?"

The duke, now enraged, prepared to attack him, but Allan saw it coming. When the man lunged, Allan knocked him in the forehead with the pistol butt. Down he went in a heap. He hurried to Marissa's side as Forbes rushed into the room, two men with him.

Allan knelt beside her. "Marissa, darling, are you well? Can you hear me? Did he hurt you?"

Her lashes fluttered. His heart leapt up in his chest.

"Allan—something—over my face—could not breathe."

"See there, men!" Forbes cried. "A dastardly crime has been attempted."

The two men gawked at the scene, the duke flat on his belly, arms outstretched, and Shaw on his back, both out cold.

"Yes, indeed," Allan agreed. "If not for Forbes, a brave fellow, my lady would have been spirited away, causing a huge scandal for Mivart's. He deserves recognition from the management. Who are you men?"

"House officers, sir. We see to hotel safety and security."

Marissa stirred.

Allan grinned, jubilant. "My lady seems to be recovering. I will take her back to our suite. I trust you will see that the duke promptly leaves the hotel?"

"Blighter is a *duke*?" one man whispered.

"A nasty one. You can readily see an even bigger scandal threatens, gentlemen. His Grace must go promptly, along with his servant, Mr. Shaw, who menaced me with that pistol over there and forced me to knock him down, as you can see. Likely the beggar wielded the chloroform and took Marissa from her room."

The fellow shifted his stance. "Aye, I smelt it roundabout. This is disgraceful."

"Gawd," the other one murmured. "This weapon is loaded. We will clear this up, sir."

The men regarded the prone nobleman with some astonishment, murmuring to themselves.

"Forbes," Allan said, "you are a hero." He handed him another sovereign, and the man beamed.

"May I help you with your lady, my lord?"

"No, I believe I can make it." Allan scooped Marissa off the sofa, her weight nothing, and walked out the ruined doors in victory, the girl securely in his arms.

"Mmmm," Marissa whispered. "I believe I can walk."

"Not with me to carry you, my love. Hang on, we have stairs to descend. Then how about some breakfast?"

****

Marissa detected no ill effects from her ordeal, except a sweet, perfumey smell that lingered in her nose.

Allan insisted she rest and busily ordered a large breakfast. They ate and drank with enthusiasm, filling every corner of her stomach, each of them relating what they knew.

"I thought it must be the maid from yesterday and answered the hall door. A wet cloth came over my face, I struck out and hit something, maybe him, Shaw, then nothing, until I woke in that room. Did you knock the duke to the floor?"

Allan munched bacon strips. "I did. Shaw, too, when he got mean. His Grace became some peeved, I must say, when I showed up. Despicable fellow."

"What will happen to him?" she asked.

"Ludlow is, after all, a duke. Likely nothing will occur but being barred from Mivart's. But the seed of his disgusting actions in a public place will grow into a vine. All such low behavior comes to light eventually."

They drank their coffee.

"Plus," Allan added, "there will be no gossip concerning us. He will not care to mention such a defeat. And he knows that we know he is an ass. He has to pray we do not drop a word in the right ear." He replaced his cup. "Shall we go on with our plan?"

Marissa hesitated, not knowing which plan he referred to. "To go to my aunt?"

"Not yet. I hardly dare to allow you to freshen up, but do so, then I want to visit a shop I noticed downstairs."

She stood. "I will not be a moment."

"Make sure that door is locked!" he called after her.

She nervously checked it. Twice. Marissa tidied her troublesome hair and washed her face and hands, her thoughts in a jumble. She dried off, picked up her reticule, and hurried back to him, slightly light in the head, wishing he would spell out what he intended, but afraid to ask.

Allan waited in the sitting room, so tall and handsome, so brave and strong, she gained courage. Had he not bested the loathsome duke, and pesky Shaw, too, and saved the day? Allan could do anything.

"Here I am," she timidly said.

"And worth the wait." He bent to kiss her lips. "You are more beautiful every time I see you."

Marissa leaned to him, mesmerized. "Whatever happens, Allan," she blurted, "I will always love you."

His charming smile. "I will hold you to it, my angel. Let us go."

They left the room, and Allan locked the doors. They strolled down the hall, her arm in his. If this signaled the end, she would strive to accept it. He had saved her from a horrid fate and word of her, um, fall from grace would never be spoken of. She would tell her aunt she had been visiting a friend and the devil take it. Then she would cash that bleeding draft and set out to make a life.

Down the stairs and into the crowded lobby. Too bad she had to leave all this glamour. Never get to dine in the restaurant and see more of the amazing people. She tried to look at all of them at once, then Allan tugged her into a shop. A hat shop!

He gazed down at her. "I said I would buy you a new hat, Marissa. Please see if you like something here."

A pert lady joined them. "Good day."

"A hat for my lady, please," Allan directed.

"Ah. Come this way, if you will. I have just the thing."

She led Marissa to a bench at a long table with the largest mirror she had ever seen. The woman presented boxes of hats, opened one, and unwrapped thin colored papers.

"Your face is heart-shaped, and your hair is glorious. The new styles from France, now that we are over that unhappy disagreement of late, dictate a move away from the bonnet toward a smaller mode."

She presented an intricately woven pale straw hat that appeared lopsided. A tiny veil adorned the tilting brim. The woman placed the hat at an angle on the top of Marissa's head, inserted a pearl-tipped pin, and stood away.

Marissa considered this view and completely adored the hat. In its plain aspect, it looked totally elegant. Allan leaned to see.

"This one," she said.

"Ohhhh?" the lady mourned. "I have many more that might suit."

"She will take that one," Allan said. "It is perfect."

Marissa adjusted it a bit, finding it most flattering. Allan dropped coins into the woman's hand, and she waved them goodbye. They left the shop.

"Thank you, Allan. It is the loveliest hat I have ever had."

"You make it lovely, Marissa." He glanced up at the lobby clock. Just past ten. "Right on time, sweetheart." He took her hand. "Come along, and we will get the license."

Marissa stumbled after him, nearly overcome. Heaven save her, it would actually happen!

The doorman raised a whistle and blew it to summon a hackney. Allan directed the jarvey and helped Marissa in. This proceeded according to plan; all his gambles were paying off. They crossed town, Marissa bent toward the window, attentive to the passing scene.

Allan kept his excitement contained but would not be satisfied until the ceremony had been properly conducted. Then he could stop fearing he would turn around, Marissa would be gone, and he would be cast back into his lonely life. The earldom would be no solace without her. The things that really mattered had all fallen into line, and Marissa had first place in the queue. How this could come about in such a short period of time perplexed him, but it seemed more actual than his own pulse and just as vital.

"I owe you that tour of the sights, Marissa. I will keep that promise tomorrow."

She held his arm. "Will you?"

"I will. What would you like to see? The Tower? The parks? The best shops?"

"Noooo. More than anything, I would love to visit the British Museum."

Such a grand woman. "An admirable goal. It shall be done."

"Everything is there, everything," she related. "I have read of the exhibitions, but to actually see them…" She drew a breath. "…has been a dream."

She talked on as Allan admired everything about her. Soon, they turned into Doctors' Commons, with its cluster of court buildings, and the offices of the Archbishop of Canterbury. The jarvey stopped the hack right by the proper door.

"I am unwilling to lose sight of you, Marissa; come with me."

"Oh, good."

They climbed down. "Please wait," Allan requested. "I will make it worth your while."

"Aye, guv."

They entered the office, which smelled of candle wax, starch, and ink. A staid fellow eyed them, and Allan stepped to the counter.

"Good day. We are here to obtain a special license."

The man resolutely withdrew a paper from somewhere beneath and pushed it toward him. The fellow offered a pen. "Fill this out, sir, front and back. There is a fee."

"I can pay." Allan ticked off questions, had he ever been married, had the bride ever been married, any reason a marriage would not be valid, and so on. He answered all the questions and signed.

The fellow read his signature and perked up. "Ah, my lord; one moment." He scurried away.

"I read it all," Marissa whispered. "It seemed safe."

Allan had to laugh but kept it quiet. Back the fellow bustled waving a paper heavy with stamps and seals. "All in order, my lord. The fee is listed if you will."

He counted out the sum and pocketed the paper.

"I do wish you well," the man said, with a watery smile.

"How kind of you," Marissa answered.

"Thank you." Allan took Marissa's hand, and they walked out. As easy as that, he moved one step closer to having her as his true and lawful wife.

Back they went to the hotel. Marissa and Allan crossed the crowded lobby, filled with the usual hubbub, and turned down a hallway just past the stairs.

The chapel lay behind a door with a stained-glass panel of a figure herding sheep. Marissa thought this appropriate, and Allan opened the door. There sat a vicar, all in black save for his white collar, seated at a table eating a plate of food.

"Oh," he squeaked, his fork in mid-air. "Is there a problem?"

"Not anymore," Allan stated. "We would like you to marry us."

"Yes, please," Marissa agreed. "But do finish your lunch. We will wait."

She and Allan sat down in two straight chairs and held hands.

The man took a few more bites. "So thoughtful of you. I relish this hour because I am given my choice of luncheon. This is a rare luxury. The housekeeper at the vicarage is a Spartan lady. Today, I have had the hotel's famous lobster salad." He scooped up a last bite and dabbed his lips with a large serviette. He stood and walked forward to a lectern, opened a book, and thumbed to a page. They followed.

"I am Reverend Woolsey. And your names?"

"The lady is the Honorable Marissa Barrington, and I am Allan Rutledge, Earl Townshend."

"With an h," Marissa added.

He laboriously wrote all this down. Allan handed him the license. Marissa's pulse beat in her ears.

"All well and good. Would you join hands? My friends, marriage is a bond that will never cease. Do enter the state with full consideration."

"Yes, we have thought it over," Marissa assured him.

"Definitely," Allan added.

Reverend Woolsey cleared his throat importantly and with no text to guide him, began the ceremony.

"Dearly beloved—"

Marissa went deaf. It became so overpowering, so unexpected, so immense, she just stared at him and tried to read his lips. Her vision blurred.

"May I have the ring?" he said to Allan in a booming voice that made her flinch. They had no ring!

But Allan lifted her hand and slipped a heavy ring onto her finger, and she looked at it. A gold signet ring, with a green stone and a crest, and the ceremony wound to a close. Reverend Woolsey now carefully made out a printed certificate, then gave it to Allan.

Allan squeezed her hand. They mumbled thanks and scampered out the door. Allan picked her up and whirled her around. "Lady Townshend. My countess."

"My husband. Oh, Allan, is it all real?"

"Yes, darling, the world is open to us. What shall we do? Have a wedding lunch in the dining room, in our room, replace that ring with one suitable for a bride, or go see the British Museum?"

"The museum can wait. Everything can wait. I would like lunch, but in our room, where we can relax." She smiled with brimming happiness. "And begin our honeymoon; no one looking for us, no disturbances. Perhaps tonight we can have dinner in the dining room and show ourselves off to the masses."

"Heavenly."

Arm in arm, they headed for the stairs and down the hall to their rooms. Inside, Allan took her in his arms.

"I love you so much, Marissa. Say you love me, too."

"I truly love you, Allan, everything about you, and believe I always will."

They kissed, a deep kiss, a kiss of commitment. This

loving went on, each of them delighted by the other, by the events of today, and yesterday, and the day before. And all the glorious days ahead.

"I have so much to show you, darling," he whispered in her ear. "So much loving to give. I will fill your every crevice with my affections."

"Yes," she murmured. "You said you would. Show me, Allan. Show me now."

He laughed and led her by the hand to the bedroom. Lunch could wait, like the museum, Marissa thought. The future calling, Allan summoned her, and she would never say no. Not ever. No matter what. Therefore.

A word from the author…

I spent my career as a painter and came late to writing. I began with contemporary romance/mystery novels, set in a small ranching community near Santa Fe. One of these novels, *Elena Chavez*, was published by Decadent Publishing.

Soon, Regency period historicals captured my interest. I strive to portray intelligent, self-aware characters, and I include a cheerful amount of sex.

Visit me at:

https://www.jeanettecollinshighdesertart.com
https://www.jeanettecollinsauthorpage.com

Thank you for purchasing
this publication of The Wild Rose Press, Inc.

For questions or more information
contact us at
info@thewildrosepress.com.

The Wild Rose Press, Inc.